THE YEAR OF KAI & ISA: VOLUME 1

(SUNNYVALE SERIES, #4)

JESSICA SORENSEN

The Year of Kai & Isa: Volume 1

Jessica Sorensen

All rights reserved.

Copyright © 2019 by Jessica Sorensen

ISBN: 9781939045270

For information: jessicasorensen.com
Cover design by MaeIDesign

ONE
ISA

*L*YNN *ESCAPED.*

Lynn escaped.

She's out there, somewhere in the world, and she could come after me at any time.

When Kai and my grandma Stephy broke the news to me, I couldn't believe it. Part of me still doesn't believe it. Or, well, doesn't want to believe it.

But, as I lie here in the hospital bed with too much time to think, it's hard to ignore, or not think about the reality

Lynn escaped.

I let out a stressed sigh then crinkle my nose as the stench of cleaner and what can only be described as old blood that hits my nostrils. I'm really starting to hate the stench of hospitals and the sounds that fill them. Like right now with the heart monitor beeping, starting to make my head pulsate. But that's not even the worst part. No, the worse is when a screaming patient got wheeled through the hallways.

It happened last night and startled me out of my sleep. I ended up staying awake for hours, wishing Kai was with me, but he had gone back to my grandma's house to get some sleep, something I had to make him do since he was starting to look sleep-deprived.

Everyone looked a bit worn out. Even myself.

God, I wish I could go back to sleep. But my mind is too wired, on edge, and filled with worry that Lynn is going to walk through those doors at any moment and burn me alive. Even with the officers stationed outside, I can't seem to relax, so I'm left stuck in this bed, wide awake, waiting for something, anything to happen.

As boredom sets in, I try to close my eyes to go to sleep, but my mind goes straight to thoughts of Lynn.

I still can't believe that, after everything, she ended up escaping and is on the run. And with my dad.

Right after the fire, I thought Lynn and my dad were for sure going to be captured and put behind bars. I'd been so close to having my freedom, and now ... well, I have no clue what awaits me now. My future is a mystery, undecided. All I know is that I have a lot of decisions to make. Decisions I'm not even sure I want to make.

One positive thing has come out of this. Lynn made a recording of when she tied me up to the bed, which included her confessing everything she did to me and her son. So, more than likely, my mom will be released from prison. Just knowing that makes it easier to breathe. Well, right now it does. Last night, when I heard the screaming in the hallway, my lungs felt very tight and, for a moment, my mind rushed back to when I was in my bedroom, flames surrounding me.

I thought I was going to die.

I thought I *had* died.

I swallow a breath, the beeping on the heart monitor increasing. I really need to get the hell out of here so I can stop thinking about what happened.

If I can just get out of here, away from the smells, beeping, and screaming, I'll be okay.

At least, that's what I try to convince myself, but deep down, a part of me worries that what happened to me might've broken something inside me, a worry that increases when I shut my eyes and all I see are images of flames and smoke.

———

I END up not falling back to sleep and, hours later, when

Kai enters my room, I feel like my brain isn't even on anymore.

"Hey," he greets me with a smile.

He looks a lot more rested than the last time I saw him, the dark circles no longer present underneath his eyes. His light blond hair is styled in this messy, bedhead way, and he's dressed in his typical style of black jeans, a matching shirt, and he's rocking a pair of Converse sneakers.

Even though I'm butt-ass tired, I manage a smile. "Hey."

A crinkle forms between his brows as he stops beside my bed. "What's wrong?"

"It's nothing," I say, not wanting to worry him. Because, if I tell him I'm exhausted, he'll more than likely feel guilty for going home and leaving me here alone.

He places a hand against my cheek, skimming his fingers across my cheekbone as he stares down at me, his eyes searching mine. "I can tell something's bothering you, so fess up." The corners of his lips quirk. "Or else I'm going to have to tickle it out of you."

I bite back a smile. "You can't tickle me while I'm on oxygen."

"Says who?" he questions amusedly.

"Um ... Says the doctors."

"I think you might be lying to me, baby."

A laugh tickles my throat as I make a gagging face. *"Baby?* For reals?"

He wrestles back a grin. "What? It got you to laugh, didn't it?" Mischievousness glints in his eyes as he casts a quick glance around the room. Then he leans in toward me.

At first, I think he's going to kiss me, which yes, pretty please with extra gummy worms on top, but then he comes to a stop, his lips inches away from mine.

I'm about to pout when he sticks his hand in his pocket. "I brought you a present," he whispers as he pulls out a bag of ...

"M&Ms!" I exclaim excitedly and probably a little too loudly.

"Shh ..." Kai whispers through a soft chuckle. "You're going to get us busted."

"Sorry. I'm just so sick of hospital food, and I haven't had anything with real sugar in it for, like, days." Since Lynn tried to burn me alive.

I swallow hard at that thought, my heart feeling a bit shaky, something the heart monitor announces.

Kai's brows knit, and he starts to turn his head toward the monitor, but before he can stress out about it, I cup the back of his head and guide his lips to mine, giving him a quick kiss. It's a bold move for me—he's usually the one who instigates all our kisses—but it distracts him from the spike in my heart rate.

"Thank you for the candy," I whisper as I pull back.

He nods, wetting his lips with his tongue as he stares at me. "I figured you were probably jonesing by this point." He cracks a smile. "You're such a little sugar junkie."

"Yeah, but it's, like, the best addiction ever. And candy is the best thing ever."

"Nah, I'm going to have to disagree with that."

I playfully narrow my eyes at him. "You know what? I don't think you, and I can be friends anymore."

"Yeah, I don't think so either," he agrees then dips his lips and seals them to mine, giving me a soft kiss. He doesn't pull back right away, lingering his lips against mine as he shuts his eyes and breathes in. "I know we haven't really had the talk about what we are," he whispers. "With everything going on, there hasn't really been time, but I think—or feel, I should say—that I don't want to be friends with you anymore."

"What?" I whisper, confused and kind of hurt. "Why?"

What the heck is going on?

"Well, considering all the kissing we've been doing, and the fact that I told you I love you ... and you said it back"—he takes an uneven breath—"I'm thinking—and I'm hoping you agree with me—that maybe we should be girlfriend and boyfriend. " He leans back and offers me an easy smile. Or, well, at first glance it looks easy, but I detect a hint of nervousness residing in his eyes.

Is he worried I'll say no? Or is that from something else?

Then I replay his words in my head and a burst of excitement rushes through me, something that gets announced on the heart monitor.

He flicks a glance at it then looks back at me, tilting his head to the side. "So, either that's a *hell yes* or a *fuck no*. I'm hoping the first one." He waits for me to respond with that smile on his face, the one that makes my heart flutter.

"It's the first one," I tell him, my tone a bit shaky.

Relief washes over his expression. "Good." He leans in and kisses me again but pulls back way too soon.

This time, I do pout.

He chuckles. "Relax. We're nowhere near done with this yet." He sits down on the edge of the bed. "It's just that your grandma drove me here, and I don't wanna be full-on making out when she comes in here ... She's already given me, like, ten lectures about treating you right, which I fully plan on doing." He winks at me.

I can't help smiling, but then confusion tap dances through me. "If my grandma drove you here, then why didn't she come in here to see me?"

"I think she's talking to the doctors about having you

released today," he explains, the smile remaining on his face, but it's no longer genuine.

No, it's fake and covering up worry.

"Is something wrong?" I ask as I tear open the bag of candy.

He swiftly shakes his head. "Everything's fine." He tucks a strand of my hair behind my ear. "We all just want to get you out of here and take you home."

I nod in agreement, and he keeps on giving me that fake smile.

"Are you sure that's all that's going on?" I eye him over suspiciously.

He nods, brushing his fingers along my jawline. "Yeah."

While I want to believe him, believe that he hasn't gone back to lying to me, I can't get past the fake smile on his face.

Because fake smiles usually only appear to conceal lies.

TWO
KAI

I'm lying to her, and I hate that I am, but her grandma made me promise to keep my mouth shut about what happened this morning until we got Isa out of the hospital. Once we have her out, then we're going to tell her.

On the one hand, I'm relieved that we are, because I hate lying to Isa. But I also know that what we're going say will stress her out even more. And that's the last thing she needs right now. After everything that's happened, she doesn't need a drop of stress in her life. Unfortunately, none of us have control over that, something her grandma and I were reminded of this morning when that stupid note showed up in the mailbox.

"You're zoning out on me," Isa says as she stares up at me from the hospital bed that she's been stuck in for days.

She still has a tube running underneath her nose, bandages on her wrists, and her eyes are bloodshot, a sign she didn't sleep very well. She's still gorgeous as hell, though, with her long, brown hair around her head as she stares up at me with her big eyes. And those lips ... Fuck, they're so tempting. I'm probably going to end up getting a lot of lectures from her grandma Stephy in the future, because there's no way in hell I'm going to be able to not kiss Isa every time I see her. That's okay, though. I'll deal with the lectures if it means I get to be with Isa.

I like that her grandma cares so much about her. Isa needs that in her life, needs to be surrounded by people who care about her. With how messed up Lynn, her dad, and Hannah have made her life, she needs easiness in the future. And I plan on giving her that. I just wish I had my shit together more.

Yeah, this whole thing with T is over, and I found a place to live, but I don't have a car or a job yet, and school is ... well, I'm barely passing at this point.

I need to get my act together, if for nothing else than for Isa.

I make the silent vow to myself then focus on Isa as she stuffs her face with a handful of M&Ms.

"Oh God," she groans as she closes her eyes.

The look on her face and the little moans escaping her

lips is making me want to kiss her again. No, scratch that. I don't want to just kiss her. I want to touch her. Feel her.

I bite down on my bottom lip as she opens her eyes, shoves another handful of candy into her mouth, and moans again.

"Good?" I ask, feeling like I'm about to explode with sexual tension.

She bobs her head up and down. "It's delicious." She licks her lips.

Someone please kill me now, because I don't know how much more moaning I can take. It's making me feel like I'm about to crawl out of my skin. And it's turning me on so much it actually hurts.

"You have a weird look on your face," she remarks as she pours more candy into the palm of her hand.

"Yeah, I know," I say. "I'm really struggling right now."

The confused look that flashes across her face is absolutely adorable. "With what?" she asks.

I dither, unsure how honest I want to be with her. Our relationship is so new that I'm not sure if I should be throwing out dirty comments yet. Although, she did let me feel her up the other night ...

My thoughts start to drift back to that moment when she lay on top of me, letting me kiss her and stick my hand up her shirt ...

"Kai?" Isa places her hand against my cheek. "What's going on?"

I blink from the memory and focus on her. "It's nothing. I'm just thinking about ..." I waver again then decide to hell with it and just be honest—be myself—because Isa seems to like that, likes who I am, something I'm still getting used to. I lean in, putting my lips behind her ear, and bite back a smile as her breathing increases. "All those little moans you keep making while you're eating the candy has me thinking about the other night when you let me touch you." I slant back, meeting her gaze, and am reward with a blush creeping across her cheeks. I sink my teeth into my bottom lip, struggling not to smile. "So, yeah, that's what's going on."

"Oh." She gives a short pause then shakes her head. "Is this how you're going to be from now on?"

I angle my head to the side. "How am I being?"

She lifts a shoulder. "I don't know ... Perverted."

I lift a brow. "You say that like I wasn't before."

She chews on her bottom lip. "Yeah, you're right. But still ... you didn't say stuff to me like you just did."

"Maybe not a lot, but I did sometimes. And honestly, I wanted to a lot, but I held back because I didn't want to freak you out."

"Oh." She rubs her lips together. "You know I'm not

totally naïve, right? You don't, like, have to censor yourself around me. You can say whatever you want."

"Careful," I warn in a playful tone. "You might want to give me free rein like that."

She rolls her eyes. "I'm not afraid of you and your pervy mouth."

I bite down on my tongue, trying to decide how far I want to take this. She seems so relaxed with the conversation, which is what I wanted, so I decide to keep going.

"All right, but don't say I didn't warn you." I dip my lips back toward her ear again and breathe lightly on her earlobe. She shivers as soft, breathy exhales rush from her lips, and a smile takes over my face. "When you make those little noises like that, I want to touch you ... I want to run my hands all over your body, feel every inch of your skin ..."

"Kai ..." she whispers shakily.

At first, I think maybe I pushed this whole verging-toward-dirty-talk thing too far, but then she tilts her head toward mine and brushes her lips across my cheek.

Sucking in an inhale, I turn my head toward her with every intention of kissing her. And not just brushing our lips together. No, I want to slip my tongue into her mouth and kiss her deeply. But then we both freeze when someone clears their throat.

"Good Lord, you two and the kissing," Isa's grandma's

voice floats across the room. "At this rate, I think I'm going to have to set some ground rules or maybe sit down and give you both a safe sex talk."

"Jesus, she loves embarrassing me," Isa whispers, embarrassment lacing her tone.

I bite back a smile as I lean back and take in her flushed face. "She's not the only one who does."

She gives me a dirty look, but the corners of her lips threaten to turn upward. "Whatever. One of these days, I'm going to embarrass you back."

I can't keep a laugh from leaving my lips. "Yeah, good luck with that."

She glares at me then rolls her eyes and turns her head toward her grandma. "So, am I getting released? Please say yes, because I'm really getting tired of this bed."

Her grandma nods. "Yep. I had to pull a few strings, but I think we're going to be busting you out of here in the next hour or so."

Isa rests her head against the pillow. "Thank God. I am so ready for things to go back to normal."

Her grandma smiles, but it looks a bit forced. "Unfortunately, the officers are going to have to follow us home." She trades a subtle glance with me before looking back at Isa. "There are some things we need to talk about when we get home, too."

Isa lifts her head, her brows knitting as she looks at her grandma. "What's wrong?"

Her grandma steps up beside the bed and takes her hand. "It's not anything major. It's just something that happened this morning that we need to make you aware of."

She's sugarcoating the truth, and I'm not sure how I feel about it. I mean, I can understand wanting to protect Isa, but eventually, we'll have to tell her the truth.

The painful, ugly truth.

I just hope to God it doesn't break her.

THREE
ISA

THEY'RE KEEPING SOMETHING FROM ME, AND IT'S driving me crazy. I'm going to get the truth out of them, but I'll wait until we get home, because I can tell Grandma Stephy isn't going to tell me anything until then. And while I can sometimes sucker Kai into telling me things, he's all about the respecting-my-grandma thing. Truthfully, I think he's just trying to impress her, the little ass kisser. I tell him that after we leave the hospital and are sitting in the back seat of my grandma Stephy's car.

"Since when are you such a little ass kisser?" I whisper to him.

He gives me an innocent look. "I have no idea what you're talking about." He drapes his arm around my shoulders and draws me closer to his side. "Relax, baby, everything's going to be okay."

I roll my eyes. "Stop calling me baby." While I try to be annoyed, the butterflies constantly living in my stomach whenever I'm around Kai flutter like a bunch of crazy, little weirdoes.

Yeah, apparently, butterflies are suckers for silly, little nicknames.

Smirking, Kai lowers his head and puts his lips beside my ear. "Don't pretend like you don't like it."

"I don't," I lie, shivering as he runs his finger along my kneecap.

"I think you do." He brushes his lips across my earlobe.

I smash my lips together and breathe through my nose to avoid gasping, which will draw Grandma Stephy's attention, and that'll probably lead to a lecture about how to put a condom on.

"Relax," Kai whispers, threading his fingers through mine.

"I am relaxed," I say. And it's the truth.

Well, it is until my gaze drifts to the rearview mirror and I spot the police car following us, a reminder of everything that has happened and is still happening.

I let out a sigh and rest my head on Kai's shoulder. "How long do you think they're going to have to follow us around like this?"

Kai runs his fingertips through the strands of my hair. "The cops?" he asks, and I bob my head up and down, exhaustion tugging at my eyelids. "I'm not sure ... I think we're supposed to go down to the police station sometime this week, so maybe we'll find out then."

My brows pull together. "Why do I have to go to the police station?"

He continues to comb his fingers through my hair. "I think the detective working the case of ... Lynn and your dad wants to talk to you."

"About what?" I squeak, panic rushing through me.

I'm not even sure why I'm panicking, other than the idea of talking about what happened ... and with someone I don't know ... a detective ...

I swallow hard as images of flames and smoke flash through my mind.

It was so hot.

And I couldn't breathe.

I thought I was going to die.

Kai immediately cups my face between his hands. "Take a deep breath," he instructs, and I obey, inhaling and exhaling, clutching the bottom of his shirt. "Good. Now take another one."

Again, I do what he says, repeating the movement until my heart settles down again.

"You always know how to handle me when I get like that," I say quietly. "When I have ... panic attacks."

I used to have them all the time when I was younger

and had to deal with them by myself. A couple of times, Hannah and Lynn actually made fun of me while I was having one. And my dad just pretended like nothing was happening, always looking the other way.

Just like he did with the murder Lynn committed.

The murder Lynn committed and blamed on my mom.

No one has given me an update on what's going on with my mom, so I'm assuming there isn't any information just yet. Hopefully when I talk to this detective, they'll be able to tell me something.

Hopefully, they'll tell me that my mom is getting released from prison.

"Thank you," I say as I look up at Kai.

He skims his thumb along my cheekbone. "You don't need to thank me for that. I didn't do anything except tell you to breathe."

"Yeah, but ..." I press my lips together, taking another breath. "It makes me feel better, not having to deal with it alone, so thank you."

"You don't have to deal with any of this alone," he assures me, looking me straight in the eye. "Ever again."

My heart quivers in my chest. Luckily, I'm not still hooked up to the heart monitor or he totally would've noticed.

"Oh, good Lord, you two are stupidly cute," my

grandma Stephy interrupts the moment in a way only she can. "It's going to make it a pain in the ass to give you lectures."

"Good," I tell her. "I'm not a fan of your lectures."

She busts up laughing as she flips on the blinker to turn into the parking lot of her apartment complex. "Oh, I didn't say it'll stop me from giving them. I just said it's going to make it a pain in the ass to give them."

I let out a dramatic groan that causes both her and Kai to chuckle.

"I don't know what you're laughing about, boy," Grandma Stephy says to Kai with a smirk. "You're going to get a lot of lectures from me, too."

Kai simply shrugs, slipping his arm farther around me and pulling me closer to him. "Totally worth it," he whispers in my ear then kisses my earlobe.

It's the perfect moment. I wish it could last forever. Wish we could remain in this little bubble of stillness forever. But deep down, I know it can't last, not until Lynn and my dad are behind bars and my mom isn't, something I'm reminded of the moment I step out of the car and my gaze strays to the police vehicles.

"Are those cops going to stay here to keep an eye on me?" I ask as Kai moves to climb out of the car. When he nods, I sigh. "Jeez, how much protection do I need?"

He pulls a wary face as he extends his hand in my

direction. "Come on; let's go inside, get you a plate of cookies, and then we need to sit down and tell you about something that happened."

Pressure builds in my chest as panic floods me, but I shove it back, reminding myself to breathe, and place my hand in Kai's, clutching on for dear life.

Because it's literally the only thing keeping me together right now.

FOUR
ISA

No one is in my grandma Stephy's apartment when we walk in, something I find odd. It also smells like cookies, something I don't find odd. And awesome.

"Where's Indigo?" I ask as I slip off my jacket and yawn. "And where are the cookies? Because my sugar addiction is going crazy right now."

Grandma Stephy lifts a brow at me as she closes the front door and locks it. "Really? Because I was under the impression that your gentleman lover snuck in a bag of candy to you while you were in the hospital."

Kia winks at me and mutters, "I'm your gentleman lover."

I crinkle my nose as I set my jacket down on the barstool. "Um, no, you're not, dude."

His brow meticulously arches. "Then what am I?"

I shrug. "I don't know. My boyfriend."

He smiles at that, like it's exactly what he wanted me to say. "And don't ever forget that."

Um, yeah, how could I forget when he's smiling at me like that?

"All right, you two." My grandma Stephy claps her hands, interrupting the moment. "Let's get straight down to business, so I can get this over with and jump into a safe sex talk."

I glare daggers at her, but she just grins.

I sigh, sinking down onto the sofa. "You never answered me about where Indigo is."

Grandma Stephy exchanges a worried look with Kai.

I suspiciously glance between the two of them. "All right, enough with the cryptic looks. I've been through a lot over the last week, so whatever it is you two are trying to keep from me, just spit it out because I can handle it." At least, I hope I can.

Blowing out a loud exhale, Kai sinks down on the sofa beside me and takes my hand. "Indigo is staying at a hotel for a couple of days."

Puzzlement spins through me like cotton candy. Only, it's definitely not as sweet. "Why?"

Kai laces his fingers through mine. "This morning, when I walked out to the mailboxes to check the mail for your grandma, I found something in there that ..." His throat muscles work as he swallows hard. "It was unsettling."

Goosebumps sprout across my flesh. "What was it?"

He trades another look with my grandma Stephy, who frowns then takes a seat on the other side of me.

"It was a photo of you ..." She bites on her lip hard. "Or, well, that's what it's supposed to be, but it wasn't really you."

My brows pull together. "If it wasn't me, then who was it?"

"Someone who freakishly looks like you," Kai explains, skimming his finger along the inside of my wrist.

While what they're saying is strange, I'm not positive what has them both acting extremely uneasy.

"Why is that making everyone so nervous?" I ask. "And why the heck is Indigo staying at a hotel?" Because I feel like that has to do with this. I just don't know why.

Grandma Stephy places her free hand over mine. "It wasn't really the photo that has everyone concerned. Well, it does if Lynn is the one who sent the photo like the police suspect. Because if it's here, then that means she somehow took a photo of a girl who looks similar to you. And with how the photo is set up ..." She breathes unsteadily. "I really wanted to protect from all of this, but I know I can't. Not with this. You need to know—I understand that. This is just ... difficult." She's not really talking to me anymore as she stares off into empty space and starts rambling to herself. Then she shakes her head and looks back at me. "The girl in the photo ... the one who looks like you, she was tied up in some dark room. And on the back of the photo ... well, there was a very not-so-nice message. It pretty much stated that Lynn is going to try to come after you again."

I gulp but don't feel that surprised. In fact, when I heard Lynn had escaped, in the back of my mind I worried she'd try to torment me again.

And eventually come after me.

Flames.

Everywhere.

I can't breathe.

I blink, shoving the images out of my mind.

"What about my dad?" I ask quietly. "Is he ...? Is he a part of this?"

Grandma Stephy offers me a sympathetic look. "We don't know yet, hon. The police are looking into it. And they're looking for both Lynn and your father. While they do, you're going to have an officer keeping an eye on you at all times. And because of the extra chaos, we all thought it'd be better if Indigo stayed at a hotel for a few days, just until everyone gets settled."

What she doesn't say is that she made Indigo stay at a hotel so she'll be safe from this—from me. I know my grandma Stephy well enough that I understand she'll do anything to protect the people she loves. It's probably driving her crazy that she can't send me to a hotel to get me away from this mess, since wherever I go, the mess is going to follow.

Reality crashes over me.

Until Lynn and my dad are captured, this is my life now.

Fear is my life now.

And Lynn is getting exactly what she wanted.

Her revenge.

But, what exactly does she have planned for me if she gets ahold of me?

"What did the message on the photo say?" I ask, fearing the answer but needing to know.

Grandma Stephy and Kai exchange another look. Then Kai squeezes my hand.

"That doesn't really matter," he tries to assure me. "All that does matter is that you're safe. And you will be safe as long as you stay with someone at all times."

I frown. "So, I'm never supposed to go anywhere alone? Like ever? What about my job? And school? I need to go back soon, or I'm going to be so far behind that I won't be able to get caught up."

"Kai will keep an eye on you at school and an officer will be parked outside during that time. I don't think you

THE YEAR OF KAI & ISA: VOLUME 1   27

should start back up until Monday, though. You need some time to recover. We can contact your teachers and see if they can email you your work," my grandma Stephy says.

I nod. "Okay, that sounds good. But what about my job? 'Cause Kai can't go with me to that."

She hesitates. "Maybe it's best that you take some time off."

"I just started working there. If I do that, I might get fired. And I just ..." I feel awful for complaining, but at the same time, I just want to have a normal life. Want to have a life that Lynn doesn't control.

She gives me a remorseful look. "Isa, I know you don't want to hear this, but it might be for the better right now if you didn't work ... The more time you stay in the house, the safer you'll be."

I smash my lips together, trying to stay calm, but this is so freakin' annoying! Lynn goes batshit crazy, frames my mom, torments me for most of my life, then tries to kill me, and yet I'm the one who still has to give up my life, which was finally starting to get good. Well, minus the issues with Lynn, Hannah, and my dad, but still ...

"I need to go to the bathroom," I mutter then jump to my feet, slipping my hands from their holds.

"Isa," Kai starts at the same time my grandma Stephy says, "Hon, I know this is hard ..."

I don't hear the rest of what they say as I rush down the hallway and lock myself in the bathroom. Then I sink to the floor with my back pressed against the door and yank my fingers through my hair.

"This is such bull crap." Tears burn my eyes, so I squeeze them shut while taking a deep breath. "After everything ... this is where I end up ... with these stupid bandages on my wrists ... And now I can't be alone ..." The tears spring free as images of flames sear through my mind.

I'm going to die.

I'm going to burn alive.

And Lynn is the one doing this to me.

She hates me so badly that she wants me to die.

Hate.

She hates me.

I am unlovable.

"Stop it," I whisper as tears spill from my eyes.

I'm talking to myself mostly. Or, well, the tears and panic pouring around inside me. I don't want to be traumatized by what happened to me. I want to be strong. I don't want to be what Lynn and Hannah always told me I was.

Weak.

Pathetic.

Unwanted.

Deep down, I know the latter isn't completely true, but the other two ... with me sitting in here, crying on the floor, maybe they're right.

Get up, Isa.

Be strong.

But, as the images of flames flash through my mind again, I curl up in a ball, breaking apart inside, any amount of strength I had left igniting into smoke.

FIVE
ISA

I'M NOT SURE HOW LONG I LIE ON THE FLOOR, OR HOW long I would have stayed there if Kai didn't knock on the door.

"Isa," he says softly from the other side of the door. "Are you okay?"

"Yeah," I lie, my voice hoarse. I can blame that on the smoke inhalation I just suffered. Really, it's from all the crying.

"You don't sound okay." The doorknob jiggles. "Baby, let me in please. I just want to talk."

There he goes with that *baby* stuff again. And like the first couple of times he said it, my stomach goes *la, la, la.* But the sensation quickly fizzles as the images of flames take ahold of me again.

"I don't want to talk," I whisper just quietly enough that I'm not sure he can hear me.

Apparently, though, Kai has superhero hearing because he says, "Okay, well, how about you come out of the bathroom? We can go into your room and watch a movie ... And I can just hold you." He utters the last part with a hint of nervousness, sounding completely unlike Kai.

While part of me wants to remain lying on the floor so I can attempt to deal with this emotional stuff in private, the other part wants to curl up against him and focus on something else.

"Can we watch a movie with zombies in it?" I ask, brushing strands of my hair out of my face as I stand up.

"Well, duh." His nervousness shifts to amusement. "What else would we watch?"

A tiny trace of a smile tugs at my lips. "Okay, fine. You talked me into it."

Before I open the door, I hurriedly wash my face, attempting to wash away the evidence that I've been crying. Unfortunately, though, when I glance at my reflection, the eyes staring back at me are bloodshot and swollen.

"Stupid waterworks," I mutter, rubbing my eyes with the heels of my hands. Then I take in my reflection again.

Something seems different about me, but I can't put

my finger on what. I mean, nothing too obvious seems out of the norm. Freckles still dot my nose, my hair is a tangled mess of waves, and I have a tiny, little scar on my brow from when Hannah hit me in the face with a stick. It was when we were kids, and she said it was an accident, which Lynn believed. But that wasn't what happened. Hannah had purposefully hit me after she found me playing with one of her stuffed animals. I didn't have any of my own, so I had taken it without permission.

Of course Lynn and my dad believed Hannah's side of the story, and I ended up getting grounded. So, yeah, I got a scar and was locked in my room for a week, all because I took a Teddy bear.

This was when I was too young to have figured out how unfairly I was being treated. I had thought I was an awful person for taking that bear without permission. Later on, I realized my parents just hated me.

Or, well, my parent hated me. As I now know, Lynn is not my mom.

I don't know my real mom.

I wonder if my real mom looks like me.

I wonder if I'll ever get to find out.

Will we ever meet when she gets released from prison?

Will she want to see me?

Or will I be a representation of something bad, like I was to Lynn?

The reality that I very well could be churns in my gut.

Sure, my real mom sent her lawyer's assistant to check up on me, but that doesn't mean she wants to see me.

"Are you coming out? Or am I going to have to pick the lock?" Kai aims for a teasing tone, but it's overlapped with stress.

Yanking my gaze off the mirror, I unlock the door and open it.

He's standing on the other side with a frown on his face, but he instantly smiles when he sees me.

"Took you long enough," he teases. "I thought maybe you'd fallen in or something."

I give him a *hardy har har* look. "I wasn't really going to the bathroom. I was just washing my face and stuff."

His gaze sweeps across my face, and the edges of his lips curve downward. He hurriedly plasters a smile on as he meets my gaze. "Washing your face and stuff, huh?" He rubs his scruffy jawline. "Do I even want to know what the stuff part was?"

I roll my eyes. "I wasn't doing anything weird."

"Sure you weren't," he teases. "You were in there for a long time, and then you come out saying you were doing stuff. That seems a bit weird, which makes you a weirdo. But I think everyone already knows that about you."

"*I'm* the weirdo?" I question, elevating my brows.

"You're the one who's standing here, being all obsessed with what I was doing in the bathroom."

That gets him to grin.

"Yeah, I guess we're both weirdoes, huh?" When I nod, his smile expands. "I guess we must be perfect for each other, then."

"I don't know about that." I aim for a flirty, teasing tone like he almost always uses on me, but I'm not sure if I hit the mark or not. "I think you might be a little too weird for me."

"Is that so?" He's all sorts of amused now.

I dazzle him with a cheeky grin. "Yep."

He shakes his head, grinning, then steps toward me and wraps his arm around my waist, placing his palm against the small of my back. "Come here," he whispers in the gentlest tone I've ever heard a guy use toward me.

"Why?" I smirk, trying to latch on to the easiness of the conversation we were just having, because I need easy right now. Otherwise, my mind is going to go back to that room where the walls are melting, smoke is circling in the air, and death is heading straight for me. "Are you going to try to rub some of your weirdness on me?"

He shakes his head as he wets his lips with his tongue, his gaze turning intense. "No, I'm going to kiss you."

My lips form an O, but not for very long as his lips touch mine.

"You always taste sugar-y," he murmurs, tangling his fingers through my hair. Then he presses me closer to him, parting my lips with his tongue.

I suck a shaky inhale through my nose then throw my arms around the back of his neck, pulling him closer. The movement causes him to stumble into me, and I lose my balance, tripping backward. He tries to steady us but fails, and we end up bumping into the wall, his body pressed against mine. I accidentally bite his bottom lip, and I'm about to apologize when he makes this noise I've never heard a guy make before, like a soft, desperate groan. Then he deepens the kiss, keeping one hand on my back while the other molds against my cheek.

He tilts my head back, kissing me so deeply that I can barely breathe. But, honestly, I don't care at the moment as I hold on to him, sliding my hands down his back and gripping the bottom of his shirt. When my knuckles graze his flesh, a shudder ripples through his body. Then he pulls back, but only to rest his forehead against mine, his chest rising and crashing as he breathes.

"Jesus," he whispers. "This is ... I don't even have words for it."

Before I can ask if that's a good or bad thing, he seals his lips to mine again, so I assume it's a good thing. And for me it is, too. Like my favorite flavor of ice cream or like eating brownie batter right out of the bowl.

The longer he kisses me, the more intense things become, to the point where I feel completely out of my element. It makes me realize how inexperienced I am and makes me wonder just how experienced he is. I mean, sure, Kai and I are close, and we know a lot about each other, including some secrets. But I don't have a clue as to how many girls he's dated, how many times he's kissed someone, how far he's gone. Has he ... had sex?

Probably.

But how many times? And with who?

"Why are you blushing like that?" he asks.

I become aware that he's stopped kissing me and is now studying me with a curiously confused look on his face.

Yeah, Isa, why do you have that look on your face?

Because you're a freak who thinks about how experienced your boyfriend is while he's kissing you.

What is wrong with me?

"It's nothing." My cheeks flame.

"It's not nothing." His gaze sweeps across his face. "That blush on your cheeks is adorable, though."

I roll my eyes then pinch his stomach.

He flinches, a laugh sputtering from his lips. "Vicious. I like it." He grins. "But it does mean I get to pay you back."

Without warning, he pinches my side.

I flinch, tucking my arm in protectively.

"Oh, no, you don't." Holding my waist, he tucks his fingers between my arm and side and starts tickling the gummy bears out of me.

Laughter burst from my lips. "Don't you dare tickle me."

"You say that like I'm not already tickling you," he teases as he continues to tickle me while pinning me against the wall.

I squirm, trying to get free, but he barely budges, lightly grazing his fingers up and down my sides.

Seeing no other choice, I tickle him back and am reward as he giggles.

"Don't you dare," he warns.

"No way. This is totally fair." I continue tickling him.

And he does the same to me.

And, for a moment, everything is perfect, just like he said.

But then my lungs tighten as I laugh too hard and a cough sputters from my lips.

The doctors warned me this might happen on and off for a few days if I breathed too hard, or in this case, laughed.

He immediately stops tickling me. "Shit. I'm so sorry. I didn't even think." He moves his hand to my back then smooths his palm up my spine as I struggle to get oxygen into my lungs. "Deep breaths, okay? You're gonna be fine."

I do what he says and breathe in and out. About thirty seconds later, the coughing stops, but my chest aches and my eyes are all watery.

Kai releases a stressed breath. "I think we should go lie down and watch that movie."

I rub my aching chest and nod.

He gently brushes his lips against mine one more time then tangles his fingers through mine and leads me to my bedroom. I feel weirdly tired as I climb into bed. After lying in a hospital bed for days, I thought I'd finally be ready to run a marathon. Or, well, run around the block.

"What movie do you want to watch?" Kai asks as he picks up the remote from off the television stand.

"Hmm ... You pick. Just as long as it has zombies in it." I get situated, fluffing the pillow and resting my head on it. Then I tell myself to wake the hell up, that this is my first day home, the first real day I get to spend with him as boyfriend and girlfriend. I need to be awake for this. But my eyelids grow heavy almost the instant I get comfortable, and I end up falling asleep before I even see what movie he turned on.

"DO you want to see what you're going to be when you grow up?" she whispers in my ear.

I try to close my eyes, wanting to be Invisible Girl at the moment, but she smacks me upside the head. My eyes pop open, and I blink against the darkness, straining to see.

"You see that over in the corner, you little shit?" She smacks me upside the head again. "That's what you're going to become if you don't obey me."

I blink several times, trying to see what she's talking about, but darkness is everywhere, and I can't see anything. I don't even know where I am or how I got here.

"I'm sorry, but I don't see anything," I whisper in a trembling tone.

She slaps me against the head so hard that I stumble forward, landing on my hands and knees, my teeth clanking together, the cold cement scrapping my skin.

"Ow," I whimper, my bottom lip quivering.

"You're so stupid," she hisses, grabbing a fistful of my hair and forcing my head in a specific direction. "Do you see it now? Or am I going to have to make you see it?"

I shiver, scared she's going to hit me again, so I nod. "I can see it." It's a lie. I can't see anything.

But I can hear something ...

It sounds like a hurt animal. A whimpering, in pain animal.

I scan the darkness, searching for it, but she yanks me

up by the hair. This time, I bite my lip instead of whimpering, wanting to be strong, wanting her to not hurt me.

"Good. Now, remember this. Remember what you're going turn out like." She starts to drag me out of the darkness. "And if you tell anyone about this, you'll be stuck down here forever. Do you understand?"

I nod, even though I don't really understand, since I couldn't see anything in the darkness. But seeing the dark everywhere is enough for me to know I don't want to be stuck down here, so I won't ever tell anyone about this. Even though I don't know what this *is.*

As she drags me from the darkness and into the light, I hear that hurt noise again, but I'm too afraid to look back, too afraid to see what she thinks I'll turn out like. So, I keep walking forward, toward the light, until the darkness begins to melt away, shifting to smoke and flames. Flames so bright they scald me, melting me away with the darkness, stealing the air from my lungs.

I gasp for air—

My eyelids snap open as I gasp. Darkness is everywhere, surrounding me, stealing the air from my lungs.

I'm going to die.

I'm dead.

This is my tomb.

I died in that fire.

I am dead.

"Shhh ..." Kai's voice floats through the darkness as he smooths his hands up and down my back. "It's okay. Take a deep breath."

Air in. Air out.

Breathe, Isa.

Just breathe.

It was just a dream.

You're in your room at your grandma Stephy's home.

Aren't I?

I blink several times until my eyes get used to the darkness and I can make out Kai's silhouette sitting beside me on the bed. His face is just a shadow, but I can almost visualize the concern in his eyes.

"I'm sorry," I say once I've gotten my breathing under control.

"You don't need to apologize for anything," he assures me, brushing a strand of hair away from my face.

"Even if I ate all the middles out of your Oreos?" I attempt to joke, but my voice is strained with stress.

He wavers as a small smile pulls at my lips. Kai and the middle of the Oreos. I've learned over the last handful of weeks that we've spent together that he gets really protective of that frosting goodness. Lucky for him, my favorite part is the cookie. Seriously, it's like we were meant for each other or something.

"Okay, you don't need to apologize for anything," he

tells me with a hint of amusement, "unless it has to do with you being an Oreo frosting thief."

I laugh, my chest aching slightly with the movement.

"Feeling better?" he asks, and I nod. He pulls me against him and grazes his lips against my forehead. "What were you dreaming about before you woke up?" he asks cautiously.

I close my eyes and rest my head against his chest, breathing in his scent—cologne mixed with soap and something else that only belongs to him. "I'm not really sure what was going on. It was a really weird dream."

"About what?" When I don't answer right away, he adds, "It's just that you were whimpering in your sleep ... I was actually about to try to wake you up, but then you did yourself."

"You were awake already?" I pull back to look up at him, and he nods. Then I glance at the clock on the night-stand. *12:51 in the morning?* I look at him again. "Why were you still awake? And how did you convince my grandma to let you stay in here with me?"

"I was working on some stuff," he replies vaguely. "And your grandma's okay with me being in here because she knows I'll protect you if something happens, which is what's most important right now. All the time, if you ask me." He pauses. "I gotta be honest with you, though."

Worry stirs inside me. "What's up?"

"Well ..." He hesitates then reaches over and flips the lamp on.

As light shines through the room, I blink a few times until my vision adjusts to the change. Then I take him in, his messy hair and bloodshot eyes.

What has he been doing while he sat in my dark room?

Before I can ask, he says, "Something happened while you were sleeping."

My worry amplifies. "What?"

He chews on his bottom lip. "Well, I guess it's not necessarily bad. At least for me. You, on the other hand, are probably going to freak out." He grows quiet, dragging out the silence.

"Kai," I gripe, scooting toward him. "Just tell me, or I'm going to buy, like, fifty packages of Oreos, lick all the frosting off all of them, and then leave you all the cookie parts."

He narrows his eyes at me. "You wouldn't dare."

"I totally would," I quip.

"All right, I'll tell you, but don't say I didn't warn you." A smirk kicks up on his lips, and suddenly, I'm worried, but for an entirely different reason. "Before your grandma would agree to let me stay the night in here, she gave me this." He digs something out of his pocket and shows it to me. And I nearly die when I realize what it is.

A condom.

"She did *not* give you that," I deny, but deep down, I know there's a chance she did.

"Oh, she totally did," he assures me, tossing the packet down on the bed between us. "She also made sure that I understood that, when something happens between us, I make sure to be careful with you and treat you with respect."

When something happens between us?

But then I get sidetracked by the bigger picture.

"Oh my God, I love my grandma more than I love cupcakes, but she seriously needs to stop with this whole ... sex thing," I mumble, scratching my arm, trying to keep myself from blushing. "I mean, it's not like we were going to have sex, especially because I was asleep."

He rubs his lips together as he observes me. "Well, I don't think she thought we were going to have sex tonight. I think she just gave it to me for the future. Not that I didn't have condoms already." He quickly clears his throat. "But yeah ... anyway ..." He clears his throat again and scratches the side of his nose, seeming squirmy.

And me? My mind drifts back to those thoughts I had earlier when we were kissing, the ones that pondered if Kai is a virgin, and if not, how experienced he is. If I were like Indigo, I'd just ask him. But I'm not like her. I'm a virgin who's only kissed a few guys and who still blushes at the sight of a condom. Because, yeah, I'm that awesome.

"So, what were you dreaming about?" Kai asks, changing the subject, something I'm super grateful for.

"I already told you that I'm not really sure what it was about." I shrug, picking at a loose thread sticking out of the comforter.

He lowers his head to catch my gaze. "Can you at least try to explain it to me?" When I say nothing, he juts out his lip. "Please, please, pretty please with frosting, and sprinkles, and sugar—lots and lots of sugar—on top."

He looks so adorable that I find my lips parting.

"It was really dark, and there was this woman there ... She was hitting me, and she kept telling me to look in the corner of the room so I could see what I was going to become. But it was too dark for me to see anything. She wouldn't accept that for an answer, though, so I lied and said I could see it, and then she dragged me out of the darkness." I press my lips together for a sprinkle-of-a-sugar beat. "I thought I heard something make a noise, like a hurt animal, but I never saw what it was ... not that it matters." I recline against the headboard. "It was just a dream, so ..." I shrug.

He nods, but his brows furrow. "You don't know who the woman was?"

I shake my head. "No. She didn't sound familiar."

He rubs his lips together, drifting off into deep thought. I wonder if he's thinking it could have been

Lynn, that I'm having nightmares about her. It wasn't Lynn, though. Unless she was disguising her voice. Not that it matters since it was just a nightmare.

"You never told me what you were doing while I was sleeping," I divert, sliding down the bed and resting my head on a pillow.

He blinks from his daze, and his gaze flicks to the nightstand beside the bed. "I was actually messing around on the computer."

Weird, since the room was dark when I woke up from the nightmare.

I push up on my elbows and look over at the nightstand. Sure enough, his computer is right there and open, but the screen is blank.

"It actually went to sleep right before you woke up," he explains, as if reading my thoughts. "I was thinking about something ... and then you started gasping ..." Worry floods his eyes. "I know the doctors said that was going to happen, but it's terrifying to hear you breathe like that." He angles his body toward me and rests his hand on my hip. "I just want you to be okay."

"I will be. But the doctors said it'll take some time before my lungs are one-hundred percent better and ready to start laughing my butt off again." I aim for a smile but don't quite get there.

He traces circles on my hipbone, brushing his fingers

underneath the hem of my shirt and along my skin, causing a shiver to spin through me like spun sugar. "I'm not just talking about your lungs ... I can see it in your eyes ... everything that's happened ... it's affecting you."

How he can read me so well is beyond me, but it warms my heart like melted caramel.

"I'll get over it eventually." Will I, though? Can you just get over something like that? "It'll probably be easier once Lynn and my dad are behind bars where they can never, ever escape again."

"I'm sure it will be," he says, continuing to trace those lovely circles on my hip. "I want you to promise me, though, that you'll talk to me about what's going on with you. From my experience ..." He trails off then shakes his head. "With this kind of stuff, with people you care about hurting you, holding it in makes it worse."

My chest aches, but not in the same way it does whenever I lose my breath. No, this ache resides deep in my heart and is connected to him.

While Kai hasn't flat-out told me everything that his dad has done to him, I've seen and heard enough to know his father has at least smacked him around a handful of times. He's never really talked about it, just gave me bits and pieces here and there, and only when I kind of pressured him into it.

"I'll talk about it if you talk about it," I say.

"Isa, I'm fine—"

I place my hand over his mouth, silencing him. "Don't be a hypocrite. If you want me to talk about what happened, then I want the same thing from you." I lower my hand from his lips. "Remember? I don't like secrets."

He swallows hard. "Yeah, I remember."

"Good." I take a slow inhale then exhale as pressure builds in my lungs again. "So, do you want to tell me what you were doing on that computer? Because I can tell you were trying to avoid telling me."

He stares at me with a strange look on his face. "You seriously can read me better than anyone I know."

"Really?" I ask, and he nods. That makes me feel kind of good inside, like maybe I'm doing something right. "Well, I'm glad since you can read me better than anyone else *I* know."

He smiles then sighs in defeat. "Okay, I'll tell you what I was doing, but you have to pinkie swear that you won't freak out." He lifts up his pinkie in front of him.

I hitch mine with his. "I promise. But now you have me nervous." Because pinkie promises are a big freakin' deal, which means whatever he's about to tell me is a big freakin' deal.

He gives my pinkie a squeeze then withdraws his hand and reaches over to the nightstand to grab his computer. He sits up then places it on his lap, tapping a few keys then glancing at me with hesitancy. "I received an email from Big Doug today," he finally says then angles the computer screen in my direction.

"What?" Okay, that so wasn't what I was expecting.

I sit up and start to read aloud the email that's on the screen.

" '*To whom it may concern*'." I glance at Kai. "That's really formal."

He shrugs. "You know how he can get. He likes things anonymous and untraceable."

"True." My gaze returns to the screen. " '*I need your help with something. Something I can't discuss via email. If you're down, meet me at The Railing tomorrow at the same time I used to do deliveries. Sincerely, Snowflake*'." I raise my brows as I glance at Kai. "*Snowflake?*"

He shrugs. "Me and some of Big Doug's other friends call him that sometimes."

"Why? Or do I even want to know?"

Amusement dances in his eyes. "Well, I want to say you do want to know, but just so I can see that blush flush across your cheeks again."

"Whatever. Don't tell me then," I say, and he smiles wickedly, like he's planning on doing just the opposite. Before he can, I ask, "So, are you going to meet up with him?" I hope he says no because, *hello*, that is the most sketchiest email ever. And Big Doug always seems a bit sketchy.

I mean, sure, he's a nice guy, but sketchy. And then there was that whole thing where he basically just went MIA, emptying out his house and not telling anyone where he was going.

"I haven't decided yet," he admits as he sets the computer back onto the nightstand. "Maybe, though."

I resist a frown. "Oh."

He cocks a brow at me. "You don't think I should go, do you?"

"I don't know." I shrug. "I mean, I get he's your friend, but the whole thing is kind of sketchy. And you just got out of that situation with T ..."

"I know," he says, returning his hand to my hip. "But I don't think this is the same thing as with T. I think he might just need my help with something, like maybe relocating or picking something up for him."

"What if it's bad, though?" I chew on my thumbnail. "What if you, like, end up getting in trouble or hurt or something?"

He searches my eyes with his brows knit. "You're worried about me?"

I roll my eyes. "You already know I always worry about you."

"Yeah, I guess." He considers something. "How about

THE YEAR OF KAI & ISA: VOLUME 1   51

this? I go see what he wants, and if it sounds at all sketchy, I'll walk away. I don't just want to leave him hanging. While Big Doug has pissed me off sometimes, he's also helped me out a few times."

I don't want him to go see Big Doug at all, yet I also sort of understand where he's coming from. If it were Indigo asking me to do her a favor, sketchy or not, I probably would do it for her.

Still ... Kai just escaped that whole thing with T. And he's already planning ... well, whatever the hell he's planning on doing to Kyler and Hannah for what they did to me. Not that he's straight-up told me that he's plotting revenge, but he's thrown out subtle hints.

"Okay, you can go." As it dawns on me how bossy I sound, I mentally roll my eyes at myself. "Not that you need my permission. I'm just letting you know that I'm okay with you going. But it's not like you need me to be okay. You can do whatever you feel is the right thing to do. I just ..." Good hell on a chocolate chip cookie, why the heck am I rambling so much?

Apparently, Kai finds it amusing, because a smile plays on his lips as he reaches out and strokes my bottom lip with the pad of his thumb. "You're really adorable when you ramble."

I roll my eyes. "I am not."

"Yeah, you are." He brushes his lips against mine and

grins. But then he frowns when I yawn. "We should get some rest."

"I feel like that's all I've been doing for days," I say as I yawn again.

"I know, but you've also been through a lot over the last few days."

"I know, but still ... All I'm doing is sleeping all the time. I know the doctors said that's normal, but I really just want things to get back to the old normal. You know, before ... the fire." Saying the words aloud make me feel like I can't breathe.

"Here. Lie down with me for a bit," he says softly.

He doesn't wait for me to respond, lying down and bringing me with him, tucking my head under his chin so my cheek rests against his chest.

I can hear his heart beating, the pace quick and unsteady, as if he's nervous.

"Your heart's beating really fast," I whisper, resting my hand on his stomach. Weirdly, his heart rate speeds up even more.

"Weird," he mutters, moving his hand to the back of my neck.

"Why is it?" I ask worriedly. "Are you feeling okay?"

"I'm actually feeling great right now." He kisses the top of my head, and I nuzzle closer to him. His heartbeat accelerates even more.

So weird. I wonder why.

I soon become distracted as he starts to lightly massage my neck. My eyelids grow heavy as any tension vacates my muscles.

"That feels good," I murmur.

"Good," he says. "I want you to feel good."

"Well, I do." And it's the truth. Right now, in this moment, everything feels okay.

I wish it could last forever, but that hope dissolves like melting taffy as I drift off into nightmares of darkness, flames and, ultimately, death.

SIX

KAI

SHE'S WORRIED ABOUT MY HEART BEATING QUICKLY; I
can tell. But she doesn't need to worry about that. The
increase in my pulse mostly has to do with being near her
and breathing in her sugary scent. It makes my body hum
with adrenaline. It's a strange as hell feeling.

I've never actually felt this way toward anyone. I've
never been in love. And that's part of the driving force
behind the plan I'm plotting with Jules. But a tiny part of
me is also doing this for myself, to pay Kyler back for all
those years he messed with my mind. The things him and
his friends made me do ... I may have told Isa a little bit
about it, but there are way more, way worse things than
just getting stuffed into lockers.

Mostly, why I'm exacting revenge has to do with what
Kyler and Hannah did to Isa. And I can tell Isa wants to

know what I have planned, but I'm not going to bring her into this. So, before the sun even rises, I climb out of bed and go into the bathroom to get dressed. Then I sneak back into her room and write her a note so she won't worry when she wakes up and I'm not there.

Hey gorgeous,

Just wanted to let you know that I have some errands to run this morning. I won't be gone for that long, but if you need anything at all, just call me.

-- Kai

P.S. You always smell like sugar, and I love it. Just wanted to let you know that.

I leave the note on her pillow then graze my lips across her cheek.

She murmurs my name but doesn't wake up. My heart speeds up at the sound, and a smile touches my lips as I turn to leave her room.

The smile fades the moment I leave the apartment and step outside. The sun is barely rising above the hills, the sky grey and dusted with darkness, but it's light enough to see the patrol cars in the parking lot where the officers are keeping an eye on Isa. It reminds me of all the shit going on right now and how vulnerable Isa is. It makes me want to turn around, go back into her room, and watch her sleep just so I know she's okay and breathing.

Seeing her that day when I carried her out of the burning house ... it messed with my head.

I thought I'd lost her.

I can't ever lose her.

But I also can't rest until I know she's safe, until *she* knows she's safe. And that means I need to take care of a few people who caused her harm and will continue to do so. Not that I'm going to go all mobster and "take care of them." No, my plan is a bit more subtle, since I don't want to end up in jail.

As I arrive at the edge of the parking lot, I glance up the street, searching for Jules's car. He's supposed to be here by now, but the road is empty, so I dig out my phone and dial his number.

"Hey, sorry, I'm running a bit late," he answers after three rings. "I had to stop and pick up that shit we needed, and Noah was in a chatty mood."

"It's cool," I tell him, sitting down on the curb. "But I think it's weird as hell a dealer was chatty. Or was he just on something?"

"He could've been. Sometimes it's hard to tell with Noah ..." He trails off. "Hey, can I call you back? My sister's calling."

"Yeah, sure."

We hang up, and I just sit there, listening to the wind blow, because that's about all that's happening right now.

Sunnyvale is a fairly small town, and it's early enough that hardly anyone is out. Even in the late hours of night, you rarely run into anyone. It's probably why Lynn had an easy time getting that photo into the mailbox, because she probably did it at night. Although the police won't officially declare Lynn was the one who did it. And honestly, I'm not convinced either. With so many officers and people looking for her, she's more than likely lying low right now. And I don't think it was Isa's dad either, since the cops are looking for him, as well. My bet is they had someone they know and trust deliver that photo to the mailbox. That fucking photo that makes my blood boil every time I think about it.

Isa's grandma and I sugarcoated how bad it was. How in it, there was basically an Isa look-alike who was bound by ropes, her shirt covered in blood. Or, well, red liquid that looked like blood. And while we're all still confused as hell how the girl looks so much like Isa, it was the message on the back of it that made me furious.

Even though Isa's grandma and I immediately turned the photo over to the police, the image is branded in my mind, along with the message. It makes me want to hurt Lynn and Isa's father and whoever delivered the message, but since I don't know who that is, I'm doing what I can. And that means I'm having Jules look into the photo more, see what info he can find on it, like maybe who was in it. And maybe who delivered it.

I have a few ideas of who already. Kyler and Hannah were Lynn's little bitches before. They should have been arrested already, but with no real evidence—at least any that's been found—they're walking around, free to do whatever they want ... like deliver shit to mailboxes.

But, as I've learned firsthand—aka, with the video that was taken of me stealing that car—you may think you're getting away with stuff, but more than likely, something, or someone, is watching. Cameras are everywhere, like the security cameras all over the apartment complex. The problem is the police looked into that already and, evidently, the security system had shorted out for several hours last night when the photo was probably delivered. That means it was either a freakish coincidence or someone with technical skills is helping Lynn. My bet is the latter.

That doesn't mean some security camera somewhere didn't catch the perpetrator doing something that could connect them to the crime. Like I said, there are cameras everywhere, including the gas stations nearby. I just have to figure out a way to get access to them. If Big Doug was here, he'd know how to do that, which makes it a really freakish coincidence that he contacted me yesterday.

Maybe when I meet up with him, I'll ask him how I can go about doing that.

"What're you doing out here?" A guy a few years older than me approaches from the sidewalk. He's dressed in a suit and tie, and his demeanor screams undercover officer, even if he does look a bit young, probably around Indigo's age.

I squint up at him as he stops beside me. "Waiting for my ride."

He eyes me over with his arms folded, a move I think is meant to be intimidating but doesn't work on me. "A ride from who? And why are you even here at all?"

I resist an eye roll. "I don't think that's any of your business."

He narrows his eyes at me then sticks his hand into his pocket and flashes me his badge. "I hate to break it to you, young man, but I'm a cop."

"Really?" Sarcasm oozes from my tone. "Then I'm guessing you're here to keep an eye on the Anders, and if you are, then you should already know that I walked out of her place like five minutes ago. That is, if you were doing your job." I stand up as Jules's car rounds the corner. "And FYI, you might want to rethink referring to a person who's, like, maybe three years younger than you, tops, as *young man*." Anger bites in my tone at the last part, because I'm right. If he was doing his job, he'd know who I am.

His nostrils flare. "I *have* been doing my job, which is why I'm over here, questioning you. Because you look awfully suspicious, Kai Meyers. And yes, I know your name because I am doing my job, which is how I also know that you currently have quite the record of misdemeanors, which makes you a suspicious candidate."

I frown. "Candidate for what?"

He shrugs, putting on a pair of sunglasses. "Now what kind of officer would I be if I just gave out that kind of information?"

I can't tell if he's messing with me because I smarted off to him or if he's being serious. And I don't stick around to ask, hurriedly climbing into the car as Jules pulls up to the curb.

The officer offers no ominous final words, but he does make a huge point of watching us drive away.

"Dude, was that a cop?" Jules asks as he makes a turn down a side road, taking us out of Officer Douchebag's view.

I nod, slumping back in the seat. "Yeah, he was there keeping an eye on Isa."

He casts me a sidelong glance. "Then why was he harassing you?"

I shrug. "To be a dick." I fiddle with the chain dangling from my beltloop. "Apparently, he knows I have a record."

"Why was he looking into your background at all?"

"Probably because the cops are looking into everyone's background who is connected to Isa in some sort of way."

"Things are really that serious, huh?" He flips on the blinker to turn back onto the main road.

"Yeah, Lynn's fucking insane. And so is Isa's dad." I cross my arms, mulling something over. "I honestly wonder, though, if they're looking into everyone partly because of the Bella Larose case."

A pucker forms between his brows. "Who?"

"Isa's mom."

"Oh." Recognition dawns across his face. "Is she going to get exonerated then? I know a couple of days ago you briefly mentioned something like that, but you were extremely vague. Not that I don't get it, but since you brought it up again, I thought I'd ask."

"I'm not sure yet ... We haven't heard anything officially, but with that video of Lynn confessing she was behind Jamison's, her son, murder ... I'm sure she will." I hope anyway. But sometimes the law can be messed up, so a small part of me is worried maybe something stupid will happen and she won't be released. That would break Isa, not that she isn't strong as hell. And she'll pretend to have it together, but I know her well enough to understand that she'd be breaking on the inside.

"Good." Relief briefly flashes across Jules's face.

"You good?" I ask, a little confused.

He nods then throws me a grin. "I'm always good, man."

"Yeah," I agree.

For the most part, Jules does seem to always be okay. But I'm not sure if that's how he really is or if it's a façade.

I haven't known him for very long, but from what I've seen, he appears to be an easygoing guy. He hardly ever speaks about his past, though. And if anyone even tries to bring it up, he changes the subject, which leaves me wondering what his story is.

"So, how exactly are we going to plant this on your brother?" he asks, changing the subject.

"I'm not sure yet," I tell him, digging out my phone as it vibrates in my pocket. "Right now, I just want to scope him out and see what his routine is." I open up the tracking app. "And we timed this about perfectly, because he just left the house."

"You put a tracking app on his phone?" Jules muses. "Nice." He sticks his hand out for a fist bump, and I tap my knuckles against his.

"Yeah, I figure this is the best way to make sure we

won't get caught." I set the phone down on the console so we can keep an eye on where Kyler is heading.

"So, you want me to follow him then, right?"

"Yeah. Let's see what he does and go from there."

"Cool." He flips a bitch and drives in the opposite direction, heading in the same direction as Kyler.

As silence settles between us, my mind drifts to all the stuff I have to deal with, and one of them I want to discuss with Jules.

"So, Big Doug sent me a random email," I say casually, even though what I said is far from casual.

Jules's head whips in my direction. "What?"

"Yeah ... I mean, it didn't say it was from him, but it was signed by Snowflake."

He laughs at that, but then his lips tug downward. "What does he want?"

I shrug. "For me to meet up with him tonight."

"Did he say why?"

"No. The email was really vague, but I'm not surprised."

"Yeah, me neither." He gives a short pause. "Are you gonna meet up with him?"

"I think so." I sit forward as we near Kyler's destination —a coffee shop on the corner of a side road, tucked in a back area of town. The place is rundown, definitely not Kyler's scene, so why is he here?

"Be careful if you do." Jules steers into the parking lot of the laundry mat that's across the street from the coffee shop and parks. "There's a bunch of rumors about Big Doug being in some serious trouble with some dangerous people." He silences the engine then reclines back in the seat, rolling up his sleeves. "I even heard a rumor that the CIA or FBI or something like that was after him."

My brows rise. "Really?"

He gives a half-shrug. "Yeah, but who knows how true it is. Still ... just be careful."

I nod. "I will ..." I trail off as the driver's side door to Kyler's car opens and he hops out.

He has his workout clothes on, so I'm guessing he's eventually heading to practice. But that doesn't explain ...

"Why is he here?" I wonder, leaning forward, watching my brother glance around.

"He looks nervous," Jules remarks.

"He should be," I say. "But I doubt he is for the right reasons."

Jules's lips twist into a smile. "He will be soon, though." He hitches his thumb toward the trunk. "You know, if he goes inside that coffee shop, it might be the perfect time to start step one in the plan. His car is parked out of the view of any windows and away from all the other cars ... We could sneak up and plant the drugs without anyone seeing us, as long as we're careful."

I mull over what he said. "I think you're on to something." I rest my arms on top of the dashboard. "But is he even going to go in? Because it looks like he's just standing there, waiting for something."

"I know, but what?" Jules questions, putting on a pair of sunglasses.

Moments later, we get our answer when Hannah's car pulls into the parking lot. She parks right beside Kyler then hops out, smoothing her hands over her blonde hair. Then she strolls up to Kyler and kisses him on the cheek.

"You know, I really don't understand why guys like her," Jules mutters as we watch Kyler frantically peer around then grab Hannah's hand and tug her toward the entrance of the coffee shop. "She's such a bitch."

"She definitely is," I agree. "Honestly, I'm not sure as many guys are into her as Hannah likes to believe. I'm not even sure my brother's into her." At least he doesn't look like he is now. He looks pissed off and tense as he ushers her into the coffee shop.

Once they're out of sight, Jules and I hop out of the car.

I put on a pair of sunglasses as I meet Jules at the trunk. He pops it open and lifts out part of the floor, revealing a secret compartment.

"Do I even want to know why you have that in there?" I remark as he grabs a small bag out of it.

He cracks an amused smile as he shuts the trunk. "I think you've known me long enough that you get that sometimes things are better left unsaid."

I nod in agreement. He's right. Like Big Doug, Jules has done some sketchy stuff. Not that I know all the specifics, but I know enough, especially since he's carrying a bag with steroids in it right now. Plus, we've stolen a car together, so ... yeah. And when I told him about step one in my revenge plan, he didn't even hesitate. He knew where to get what I needed, and I wasn't that surprised.

I am a bit nervous, though, over what we're about to do.

Like Officer Douchebag said earlier, I have a bit of a record. Nothing serious yet. But possession of steroids ...? Yeah, that might be the final straw that'll get me either put on probation or maybe even jail time. And this time, my parents won't help me out. The only reason they ever did before was for appearances. But my dad made it clear when he kicked me out of the house that I was no longer part of the family, so whatever I do now is my problem. Not that my dad just bailed me out of things before without giving me consequences. No, my ass got beat whenever I screwed up.

"So, after we put this shit in his car, how do you want to make sure he gets busted?" Jules asks as he slings the bag over his shoulder.

"Well, I don't want to call the cops," I say. "Because, for now, I just want him kicked off the team ... I want to drag this out for him and make his life fall apart bit by bit." Torment him, like he used to torment me. And like how he helped Lynn torment Isa.

"I like your style," Jules states as we cross the street. "You know, there are a lot of things you could do with that way of thinking."

I cast him a curious glance. "Like what?"

He shrugs, adjusting the handle of the bag higher onto his shoulder. "Stuff like what I do."

"Yeah, but I'm not even certain of what you do."

"I know. We're probably gonna have to a have a talk about it soon since you'll be my roommate and some of the stuff I do is going to have you asking questions."

"Well that's ... creepy." I glance around, noting a few security cameras nearby and make a point of staying out of their range.

Jules tracks my steps, not asking questions, probably because he's thinking the same thing. "It's not creepy. Just ... weird."

"Creepy. Weird. It's all the same if you ask me." I slow to a stop as we reach Kyler's car.

My gaze sweeps the parking lot, and then I dig out my lock pick from my pocket. "After we put these in, and I'm certain Kyler's at practice, I'll call his coach and make an anonymous report that he has steroids in his trunk. More than likely, Kyler will probably try to prove to him that the call was a fake. Then he'll get an awesome surprise when he opens the trunk."

Jules slides the handle of the bag off his shoulder. "You really think he'll be confident enough to just open the trunk in front of his coach?"

"Yeah, I am." Because, while my brother and I may not be BFFs, there is one thing I do know about him.

He's an arrogant mother effer.

And that confidence is going to be his downfall.

A couple of seconds later, I get the lock picked and Jules hurriedly tosses the bag into the trunk. Then we quickly walk away before anyone can catch us.

"So, now what?" Jules asks after we've climbed back into his car.

"Now we go sign those papers for our new place," I say, fastening my seatbelt. "And while we do that, I'll keep an eye on the app. Once I know he's at practice, I'll call his coach."

"Sounds like a plan." Jules puts on his seatbelt then steers out of the parking lot. "I do wish I could find out why he's having what looks like a secret meeting with Hannah Anders on what I'm guessing they both consider the shitty side of town."

"My bet is they chose this side of town so they

wouldn't run into anyone they know." I eyeball the coffee shop as we drive by it. Through the windows, I can see Hannah and Kyler sitting at a booth, having what looks like a very heated conversation. "But yeah, I'd really like to know what they're up to, too." Because, from what Kyler told me, the last time Hannah and he were together, they buddied up to kidnap Isa. So, I can't help wondering—and worrying—about what they're up to now. I just hope that step one to my plan will stop whatever they're trying to put in motion.

That thought haunts my mind continuously until my phone pings with an incoming message. I glance down, expecting it to be a text from Isa. Weirdly, it's an email.

As I open it up, a bit of worry seeps through me. It's from Snowflake, aka Big Doug, and the subject of the email is *time changer*.

I know what that means. Big Doug used to use the term all the time when he would randomly switch up meeting and delivery times. He would do it to throw off anyone who was keeping an eye on him, which not only means he thinks someone is keeping an eye on him; it also means that he's about to change up our meeting time, something confirmed as I read the message.

"Shit," I mutter with a frown.

Jules flicks a sidelong glance at me. "What's up?"

I scratch my arm, debating what to do. I mean, I know

I've already decided I was going to meet up with him, but that was when the meeting was scheduled at night. Now he wants to meet in broad daylight, which seems risky, at least to me. But Big Doug is probably one of the most careful people I know, so ...

"Can you drop me off near the bridge after we sign the lease?" I ask Jules. "There's something I need to take care of."

I just hope I'm not making a big mistake.

SEVEN
ISA

I wake up to an empty bed and automatically assume my grandma Stephy must've kicked Kai out of the room. But then I find a note on my pillow. As I read the *P.S.* part of it, a giddy, stupidly girly smile tugs at my lips. But then I frown as I wonder what errands Kai's running.

Reaching for my phone on the nightstand, I send him a text.

Me: *Hey, just woke up and found your note. What are you doing?*

As soon as I send it, I worry that maybe I'm being too clingy, which makes me irritated with myself. I don't want to be self-conscious, but this whole boyfriend/girlfriend thing is so new to me.

"I really need to talk to Indigo," I mumble as I climb out of bed.

The moment I stand up, a message buzzes through.

Kai: *I'm with Jules right now, signing some papers for our new place. I have to go job hunting, too, but I'll try not to be too long, because I wanna see you so badly. And FYI, when you mumble my name in your sleep, you sound sexy as hell.*

My cheeks warm as I read the last part.

Me: *Whatever. That so did not happen.*

Kai: *Oh, it totally happened. And like I said, it was hot as hell. I think I need to lie in bed by you all the time so I can hear it every night.*

I roll my tongue in my mouth, feeling way out of my element, but also stupidly giddy.

Kai: *All right, I gotta sign papers now, so we have to put this sexy talk on pause. See you soon, gorgeous.*

I shake my head, my heart acting like a lunatic inside my chest.

So, this is how things are going to be with him now that we're dating? All flirty and fluttery? Really, I'm not that surprised. Kai has always been a bit flirty. I've just never had it directed on me full force. It makes me feel like I just stepped onto some new path, one paved with kisses and touching and exploring, excitement buzzing inside me to see where this is going.

Of course that excitement fizzles as I walk out of my room and find Grandma Stephy and a couple of officers sitting at the kitchen table. Then reality bitch-smacks me across the face. Hard.

I almost back out of the room, partly because I feel intimidated and partly because I'm rocking a pair of pajama bottoms, an old tank top, and my hair is a mess. But then my grandma catches sight of me and motions for me to come over.

"I'm glad you're awake," she says as I pad over to the table and take a seat beside her. "I made breakfast for these lovely officers. And for you, too." She smiles at me. "I even put extra sugar in the waffles, just the way you like it ..." She trails off as her phone rings.

I smile then start stacking my plate with waffles while Grandma Stephy walks out of the kitchen to answer the phone call.

"That's why it tasted so sugary," the older of the two officers remarks with a smile. He looks around his late twenties with blond hair, and his smile seems kind.

The other officer, however, looks like he's pissed off at the world. He also looks young, maybe around Indigo's age. He's good-looking, though, with short brown hair and hazel eyes. But the scowl kind of ruins it.

"You shouldn't eat so much," he informs the other guy, who I'm guessing is his partner.

His partner smiles amusedly. "Why not? Afraid I'm going to have a sugar overdose."

Mr. Grumpy Pants frowns. "No. I'm worried we're going to have to chase someone down and you'll get a stomach cramp from eating too much," he says, which seems kind of ludicrous until he adds, "Like you did last time."

Blondie pulls a *whoopsie* face. "All right, I won't eat anymore." He frowns then smiles at me. "So, since no one here is making any effort to introduce us, I'll do it. Hi, I'm Liam."

"She doesn't need to know anything about us, other than we're here to protect her," Mr. Grumpy Pants interrupts.

Liam just ignores him. "And this Debbie Downer over here is Holden. Although most people just refer to him as the asshole who ruined their day."

I bite back a smile as Holden scowls at Liam. "It's nice to meet you both. Well, minus the circumstances we're meeting in."

Liam offers me a sympathetic look. "I know this has to be difficult for you, but I assure you that me and Holden and all the other officers working your case won't let anything happen to you." Holden starts to say something, but Liam talks over him. "And, if at any time you can think of anything that'll help us find Lynn and Henry Anders, please let us know. And please let us know if anything happens that you feel is a threat."

I nod, relaxing a bit. "Okay, I can do that."

"We also need you to be extremely careful," Holden states in a way less compassionate tone. "No sneaking out to parties or anything that will jeopardize your safety. I know you're young, but we need you to act responsibly. This isn't a joke. Lynn Anders is a dangerous woman who's made several threats to you and has tried to harm you. And we have no doubt that she'll try again if she gets a chance."

And all my tension returns as flames flash through my mind. *I can almost feel my skin melting. I'm going to die.* "I understand that."

Liam shakes his head then rolls his eyes before standing. "Come on; let's get you back to the car before you say something else that'll scare the poor girl." He offers me an apologetic look then ushers Holden toward the door.

"Sorry about him," Liam says to me. "He has absolutely zero people skills."

Holden throws him a dirty look as he opens the door. "I do not ..." His words fade as Indigo appears in the doorway.

She's wearing a pair of yoga pants and a hoodie, her hair pulled into a messy bun.

She takes one look at Holden and that flirty smile I've seen her use a ton of times tugs at her lips. "Who are you?"

"I'm an officer of the law, ma'am," Holden replies, apparently unfazed by Indigo's smile.

"Oh." Indigo's eyes glint with amusement. "If that's the case, then where's your uniform?"

"I'm an undercover detective," Holden states like it should be obvious.

"Well, that's a shame." Indigo's tone is all flirtatious amusement. "I bet you'd look hot in one."

Instead of saying anything, Holden just walks out.

Indigo juts out her lip. "Man, I must be losing my touch."

"Nah, Holden just has issues," Liam explains as he steps out the door. "Don't take it personally." Then he hurries after Holden.

"So, that cranky piece of man candy's name is Holden, huh?" Indigo muses as she closes the front door.

I nod, relief sweeping over me. "Yeah. He seems intense."

"For sure." She pauses, looking at me for a moment. Then she walks over to me. "I'm so glad you're out of that stupid hospital."

I stand up, and she pulls me in for a hug.

"Me, too," I agree.

We hug for a moment then pull back and sit down at the table where she starts busying herself with stacking waffles on her plate.

"Sorry I wasn't at the hospital when you were released," she apologizes as she douses her waffles in syrup. "I wanted to be, but everyone thought it'd be better if less people went so there'd be less chaos. It's part of the reason they suggested I stay at a hotel for a couple of days." She sets the bottle of syrup down. "I tried to argue that I never cause chaos, but no one seemed to believe me." Her lips quirk.

I smile as I take a bite of my waffles. "What a bunch of crazy weirdoes."

"For sure." She picks up a fork but doesn't dive in, pausing to look at me. "How are you doing? I mean, I'm sure everyone has asked you that, but I know you well enough to know that you probably fed them a bullshit lie that you're fine, when really, there's no way you can be."

"I'm fine," I try to lie, and when she gives me a *really* look, I sigh. "Well, I'm as fine as I can be in the situation." When her lips part, probably to ask more questions, I stop her. "Honestly, I'm kind of tired of talking about how I feel."

She nods, cutting into her waffles. "All right, I'll take the hint." She pops a bite into her mouth. "So, what do you want to talk about?"

I shrug, reaching for the bottle of syrup. "Anything that's not related to Lynn, my dad, hospitals, fires, or police."

"Okay." She wavers as she chews. Then a grin spreads across her lips. "I know what we can talk about." A mischievous sparkle twinkles in her eyes. "Let's talk about Kai and how he's now your ..." She leaves the silent question hanging. And while I have a feeling she's going to try to embarrass me about something, I'll take that over talking about Lynn and fires any day.

"He asked me to be his girlfriend yesterday," I inform her as I add more syrup to my stack of waffles.

"And what did you say?"

"Well, yes, obviously."

"Oh, obviously," she mocks. "How can anything be obvious with you two after I spent the last month watching you guys flirt, yet every time I asked you about it, you denied you had a thing for him?"

"Hey, I admitted it eventually."

She rolls her eyes. "Yeah, but it took you forever."

I sigh. "Yeah, I know." And while I lay in that room, surrounded by flames, I thought I had missed my chance to tell Kai how I feel about him.

Luckily, I got a second chance. I just wish I knew what I was doing.

"It is a little weird, though," I admit as I stuff my mouth with waffles.

She arches her brow. "What is?"

I shrug. "This whole boyfriend/girlfriend thing. I mean ... I don't really know what I'm doing."

"That's okay," she assures me. "You'll catch on. Plus, I don't think Kai's that experienced in the whole girl-friend/boyfriend department either. At least, not from what I've picked up."

"Yeah, I've never really seen him dating anyone either." I pause, chewing on my bottom lip. "But I'm sure he's had some experience with ... stuff."

She bites back an amused smile. "What sort of stuff?"

I roll my eyes. "You know what I'm talking about, so don't play dumb with me."

She chuckles. "No way. I'm totally clueless, so fill me in." She stabs her fork into her waffles and waits with an amusing smile on her face.

"Whatever." I shake my head. "It's just that I don't know that part about Kai." I pop another chunk of waffle into my mouth. "I mean, I know a lot about him. I even know some of his secrets. But I don't know ... like"—*For the love of all Hot Tamales, just spit it out, Isa*—"if he's ever had a girlfriend or ... how far he's gone ... Like, if he's had sex," I mutter the last part. When she tries not to laugh, I swat her arm. "Don't laugh at me," I say, but as a laugh bursts from her lips, I find myself laughing, too.

"I'm sorry," she says after her laughter settles down. "It's just so funny sometimes watching you squirm like that. It's the one thing I could never teach you not to do. That's okay, though. You wouldn't be you if you didn't get all squirmy like that over sex talk."

I scratch my wrist, feeling a bit squirmy like she just implied. "I'm not squirmy ... I just ..." I sigh. "This is all just so new to me. And while Kai and I were kissing, I couldn't help thinking about how I have no clue how experienced he is and what he expects from me."

Her expression softens. "Kai doesn't expect anything from you, other than for you to be yourself. And that's how things should be in a relationship."

I nod. "I know, but I still kind of wish I knew."

She shakes her head. "You say that now, but sometimes it's better not knowing." I'm not sure if I agree with her, and she must read that all over my face, because she says, "If it bothers you that much, you can always just ask him." When I shake my head, she adds, "Or we can play a game of I Never. That's always my second plan for whenever I want to find out someone's secrets."

"You say that like you're always trying to find out secrets about people."

She gives a shrug, tension suddenly flowing off her. "Well, you know how nosey I can get."

I give her a funny, puzzled look.

While Indigo may sometimes try to pry information

out of me, she always backs off whenever I ask. And I've never thought of her as nosey.

I'm about to point all this out and ask why she looks so tense all of a sudden when Grandma Stephy enters the room.

"Isa, I ..." She struggles to get the words out, which is completely unlike Grandma Stephy, and my anxiety makes a grand appearance. "The phone ... It's ..." She takes a breath as she approaches the table and holds it out to me. "It's your mother, sweetie. She ... She wants to talk to you."

For a heart sputtering moment, I think I've heard her incorrectly. But as I replay her words inside my head, I drop the fork I'm holding.

"My mom ...? She's on the phone?" I have to double-check.

Grandma Stephy nods, and Indigo whispers, "Holy freakin' crazy troll babies."

Holy freakin' crazy troll babies is right.

I gulp and start to reach for the phone, but then I draw back as nervousness seizes ahold of me.

"I don't ..." I can't find the words to express the fear I'm feeling.

What if she doesn't like me?

"Sweetie, you don't have to talk to her if you don't want to," Grandma Stephy stresses with her hand placed over the phone. "But I really think you should. It might take one worry off your mind. Plus, you're going to want to hear what she has to tell you."

"But, how is she even on the phone?" I scratch my head. "I mean ... isn't she in prison?"

She offers me the phone. "Why don't you ask her and find out?"

"If you don't, you'll probably regret it," Indigo adds with a pressing look.

She's right.

They both are.

Sucking in a preparing breath, I reach out with trembling fingers. Then I put the phone up to my ear and utter, "Hello?"

Silence stretches across the line, and my fear soars.

She doesn't even like the sound of my voice.

Then I hear the faintest, "My little superhero girl."

The name triggers a memory so faint and worn, like a flimsy old photo tucked away in a dusty trunk.

"Come on, my little superhero girl!" my mom calls out to me as I spin in circles in the backyard with my cape blowing behind me. "It's time to go see her."

I smile and slam to a stop, so excited ...

I just can't remember what the excitement was about. I can't remember who we were going to see. All I know is that whoever it was, I wanted to see her.

"Mom," I whisper, tears pooling in my eyes as emotions pour through me, some I'm not certain I've ever felt before.

"Hey," my mom's voice floats through the line. And I recognize it, yet I don't.

It's strange. And exciting. And terrifying.

As more tears fill my eyes, I try to suck them back, but a few manage to escape.

Grandma Stephy's eyes start to water, and she quickly turns around, hurries into the kitchen, and starts busying herself with cleaning up the dishes she used to make the waffles.

Indigo gets up, too, and joins Grandma Stephy in the kitchen, helping her clean up. But she's never been one to voluntarily clean, so I'm assuming it's more to give me some privacy to talk to my mom.

My mom.

My mom is on the phone with me.

And I've barely said a word.

But I can't think of what do say.

Can barely think at all as so many emotions course through me.

"I know this must be a little strange for you," my mom finally says after silence ticks by.

"It is a little bit," I admit, chewing on my thumbnail. "I'm not really sure what to say."

"That's okay," she assures me. "I don't really have a lot of time. Honestly, the only reason I was able to call you is because my lawyer pulled some strings, and I ..." She gives a short pause. "But anyway, yeah, I'm lucky I get to call you, but I have to make this a quick conversation, even though I don't want to."

"I understand," I say, trying to reassure her.

"But I don't want you to have to understand," she mumbles. "I don't want you to have to be going through this at all ... I wish you never had to go through any of it ... I can only imagine ... after what happened ... what your childhood must've been like ..." Her voice cracks with pain.

I don't want her to be in pain. I want her to be happy.

I want her to be free.

"It's okay. My childhood ... it wasn't that bad," I say, causing Indigo and Grandma Stephy to flick a glance in my direction. But part of me feels like I'm telling the truth. That, while a lot of crappy things happened to me when I was growing up, it could've been worse.

Not wanting to endure their stares, I turn around in the seat and fix my gaze on the window.

"Oh, my little superhero girl," my mom says softly. "I know there's no way that could be true ... after what that awful woman did to you."

"It's fine," I lie, not wanting her to be sad.

"Oh, sweetie." She sighs as if just realizing something truly depressing. "I know that's not true, but we don't need to get into the details of that right now. We don't have time, unfortunately. But one day, hopefully soon, we can sit down and you can tell me everything. The whole un-sugarcoated truth."

I nod, even though she can't see me. "Does that mean you're getting let out of prison?"

"Nothing is officially yet," she tells me quickly. "But with some new evidence that has come forward, there's a very good chance that I'll be exonerated. It'll take a little bit, but the evidence ... it should prove my innocence. Because I'm not guilty. I swear I'm not, no matter what Lynn and your father told you."

"I know that." But her being so persistent to reassure me makes me wonder if she saw the video Lynn made. Isn't that the evidence that can free her? "The evidence ... It's a video, right?"

"It is ... I haven't seen it yet, but ..." She pauses. "How do you know what it is?"

I hesitate. If she hasn't seen it, then she doesn't know how badly things got for me. I wish I could make things stay that way for her.

"It's ... Well, I think I'm in it," I say. "The video, I mean."

"Oh." A pause. "My lawyer didn't tell me that. He just

said it was Lynn confessing." Another pause. "What is it? I mean, how were you a part of the video?"

I deliberate whether or not to tell her, whether I want her knowing about how Lynn tried to burn me alive. But I guess she'll find out eventually, so ...

"Time's up, Bella," someone says in the background.

"Shit," my mom mutters. "All right, just give me a second."

"Make it quick," the male voice warns. "I already let you have a minute extra."

"Yeah, okay," she tells him then mutters under her breath, "Stupid idiot thinks he's so badass, even though he's got what I'm hoping is chocolate smeared all over the ass of his pants."

I choke on a giggle. "He does?"

"Oh yeah, he does," she tells me. "Jerry—that's the asshole's name—he's a guard here and literally has some sort of stain on the ass of his pants almost every single day. Me and some of the other women in here have started placing bets each morning on what color stain he's going to show up with. It's wild fun, let me tell you." A bit of sarcasm oozes into her voice. She hastily clears her throat. "I'm so sorry. I didn't mean to come off so bitter. And I don't ever want to be like that around you. When I get out of here, I want to try to have a normal mother/daughter relationship."

"I want that, too," I say excitedly then realize she said *try*.

What does that mean? That she's worried that might not happen?

"Bella, get off the phone," the guard warns again, causing my mom to curse.

"I'm sorry, but I have to go," she says to me. "I'll try to call you again. Until then, I'll have my lawyer call and give you updates, okay?"

"Okay," I say then grow quiet, unsure what else to say.

Do I say I love you? I know she's my mom, and I want to get to know her more than I've wanted anything else, but I don't know her, so uttering those words to her ... it feels strange.

She must think so, too, because she says, "Talk to you soon, my little superhero girl." And then the line goes dead, either because she hung up or Jerry and his crap-stained pants hung up the phone on her.

As I move the phone away from my ear, I convince myself it's the latter; or else I have to accept that my mom hung up on me.

"Is everything okay?" Grandma Stephy asks from just behind me.

I take a discreet breath, collecting myself before turning around. "I think so. She just wanted to call to tell me about the new evidence found and that there's a good chance she'll be getting out of prison."

"Yeah, she told me that, too." She presses her lips together, eyeing me down like a hawk. "Is that all she said?"

I nod. "Yeah, pretty much. Well, that and she was sorry about what I had to go through. And that, when she gets out, we're going to sit down and talk about everything." I scratch my wrist, unsure of why I feel twitchy for some reason. "She also mentioned the guard there always has stains on the butt of his pants. Apparently, today it was shit brown."

Grandma Stephy's brows rise to her hairline while Indigo snorts a laugh.

"Dude, she's just as big of a weirdo as you," Indigo remarks as she opens the fridge door.

That gets me to smile, but then confusion webs through me.

Do I want to be like my mom?

I don't know her.

I don't know anything about her.

Grandma Stephy assesses me with concern. "Are you sure you're okay?"

I give my best convincing nod, but I'm not even sure who I'm trying to convince.

Everyone else. Or myself.

I frown at the thought as my phone buzzes in my hand. I glance down, only to realize I'm still holding my grandma Stephy's phone.

I move to hand it back to her. "Here—"

"Oh, for the love of hell," Grandma Stephy abruptly cuts me off, her gaze darting to the window. Then she stalks off, crossing the kitchen, striding for the front door.

I spin around in the chair, half-expecting to see Lynn standing outside the window. Nope. The only person out there is an eighty-something-year-old woman wearing a large brimmed hat and a flowery dress.

"Who's that?" I ask in confusion.

My grandma Stephy either ignores me or doesn't hear me as she storms out the front door and toward the woman.

"You have some nerve showing your face here after what you did to my cookies at the goddamn banquet." Grandma Stephy stops in front of the woman, close enough to invade her personal space, and crosses her arms.

"I didn't do a damn thing," the woman snaps, getting in Grandma Stephy's face.

I cast a glance at Indigo, who's gawking out the window now.

"What the heck is going on?"

Indigo shrugs, popping a couple of chocolate chips

into her mouth. "I have no idea, but old people fighting is freakin' hilarious."

I'm about to agree with her because it is sort of amusing watching the two of them get up in each other's faces, the brim of the woman's overly large hat bumping into Grandma Stephy's face, but then the woman suddenly throws down her cane and slams her hands against Grandma Stephy, shoving her back.

"Shit," Indigo curses, scrambling for the door as Grandma Stephy recovers her balance and charges toward the woman, her nostrils actual flaring.

I jump to my feet to go help Indigo break up the fight, but halfway across the room, my foot catches on the edge of the shelf and I stumble forward. I still have Grandma Stephy's phone in my hand and, as I start crashing toward the floor, I decide to drop it so I can use my hands to stop myself from faceplanting.

As I land on my hands and knees, the phone hits the hardwood floor with a smack. And of course it's screen down, because isn't that always the case?

"Please don't let the screen be cracked," I whisper as I kneel and pick up the phone.

I let out a breathe of relief at the sight of the crack-free screen. But my relief is short-lived as move to close the photo app that opened up during the fall.

I don't really mean to look. I mean, it's not like I was

purposefully snooping. But as my gaze briefly skims across the row of photos that popped up, one snags my attention.

A photo that looks like me, sitting in the dark, with a bunch of red crap all over my shirt. Red crap that looks like blood.

But it's not a photo of me—that much I know—which means it has to be a photo of that picture someone left in the mailbox. Kai mentioned the girl in it looked a lot like me, but I hadn't pictured the girl to look so strikingly similar. Sure, her eyes are a different color, and her hair is a bit darker than mine, but her facial features nearly mirror mine.

Who the hell is this girl? And why does she look so much like me? Better yet, what was the point of sending the photo?

Kai said there was a note on the back, but as I scroll through the photos, I don't find a picture of the note. That means, if I want to find out, I'm going to have to get the truth either from Grandma Stephy or Kai.

As I turn around to head outside where Indigo is currently dragging a red-faced Grandma Stephy away from the old woman, I decide Kai is the best option.

I just hope he doesn't go back to omitting the truth from me.

EIGHT
KAI

THE PLACE WHERE BIG DOUG WANTED ME TO MEET
up with him is a sketchy as hell area tucked underneath a
graffitied overpass and beside a grimy pond that makes the
air reeks of mold. An old barrel and a tent are off to the
right, and what looks like a body bag is just off to my left.
I'm hoping it's just a large duffel bag. Yeah, that has to be
what it is.

And that's what I'm convincing myself when Big
Doug steps out from the shadows of a cluster of nearby
bushes. He has a hood pulled over his head, casting a
shadow across his face, hiding his features. But Big Doug
is a very large dude—hence the nickname—and his bulki-
ness makes him easy to recognize, which is really unfortu-
nate for him since he's been in hiding for who the hell
know what reason.

Maybe I'm about to find out.

"Hey," I greet as I start toward him.

"Hey." He gives a panicked glance around as he nears me then starts to lift his hand.

I lift mine, too, thinking he wants a high-five, but then footsteps thud from behind me and every single one of my muscles wind into knots.

"Sorry," Big Doug mutters with an apologetic look.

"Shit." I start to spin around, but I'm slammed from behind.

As I stumble forward, I find myself wishing I'd brought some sort of weapon. But then my gaze falls on the asshole who slammed into me, and my worry shifts to confusion.

Tall and bulky, the dude is dressed in all black and has a pair of handcuffs in his hand.

An undercover cop?

Why would Big Doug be working for an undercover cop?

Or maybe he's not an undercover cop and is just some weirdo who's about to try to do who knows what with those handcuffs. Let me stress the *try* part.

I prepare to bolt. I'm not super strong, but I'm hella fast. At least, that's what my old coach used to say all the time, back in the day when I actually gave a shit about sports.

"Don't try to run," the asshole with the handcuffs warns. "As long as you don't, I won't cuff you."

I step back but tense as I feel Big Doug crowding my space.

I grit my teeth, curling my fingers into fists. I should've listened to Isa and never agreed to meet Big Doug.

"What the fuck is this?" I growl out.

The asshole in front of me has the audacity to smirk. *The fucker.*

I'm one step away from throwing a punch at him when he says, "Kai Meyers, I'm an undercover agent, and I'm arresting you for auto theft, computer hacking, and illegal possession of drugs." He reaches into his pocket and flashes me his badge.

My stomach ravels into knots as I swallow hard. "I haven't done any of those things," I lie. At one point or another, I've done all those things. But it's been a while ... since Isa came into my life.

The officer smirks. "That's what all criminals say." He holds up the handcuffs. "Now, you can come with me, or I can cuff you and drag you to my car. It's your choice."

"Just go with him," Big Doug mutters from behind me.

I have no idea why he turned me in like this and set me up, but it doesn't fucking matter. I'm still pissed off. More than pissed off.

He just ruined everything good I got over the last month.

I glare at him, wanting to punch him in the jaw.

He has the nerve to look remorseful, but that only makes the urge to punch him grow.

"You and I, we're done. Don't ever talk to me again," I say then turn to the officer. "I'll go with you."

"Smart choice." He lowers the cuffs then nods for me to go with him as he starts toward the street.

I follow, pissed off at Big Doug and pissed off at myself for ever doing anything that would get me in this sort of mess.

So, this is what it feels like for the past to catch up with you.

Yeah, the past is a nasty little bitch.

NINE
KAI

THE UNDERCOVER AGENT DRIVES YOUR AVERAGE, RUN-
of-the-mill car. He makes me sit in back and won't answer
any of my questions. Big Doug doesn't ride with us, and I
swear to God if I ever cross paths with him, I'm going to
kick his ass. Yeah, I may not be much of a fighter, but Big
Doug is an even worse one than I am.

Of course, my kicking-ass revenge plan gets shoved to
the side as the undercover agent pulls up to an old
building located on the edge of town near the foothills.

"Why are we not at the police station?" I ask, my guard
instantly going up.

When the officer says nothing, simply parking in front
of the building, I discreetly reach to the side to try to open
the door, but it's locked.

I ball my hands into fist, preparing to fight.

"Will you relax?" the officer says as he shuts off the engine. "I'm not part of the local police department."

Huh? "Then what are you?"

"I work for the DEA," he tells me then hops out of the car.

I sit in the back seat, stunned. Why the hell did the DEA arrest me? I mean, sure, he said he was charging me for drug possession, but the only amount of drugs I've ever carried on me is enough for myself. However, T may have been involved with some trafficking, and I had a connection to him.

Is that what this is about?

Before I can delve too deeply into that theory, the agent opens the door for me to get out.

"If you try to run, I'll tase you," he warns as I climb out.

Part of me wants to try to see if he'll follow through with that threat, while the other part doesn't want to get in any more trouble than I already am. I just got out of trouble, and now I am back in it again, only days later. Only, this time, instead of dealing with the drama of a drug dealer, I'm walking into a massive warehouse building with an undercover DEA agent. Honestly, I'm not sure which one is worse.

"Have a seat, Kai Meyers," the agent instructs when we reach a table set up in the middle of the warehouse.

For the most part, the space is fairly bare, except for

some crates in the far corner. The windows are grimy, including the skylights, but a bit of sunlight manages to slip in, a good thing since none of the lights are on.

Even though my initial reaction is to rebel, I swallow the urge to smart off and take a seat at the table.

The agent rolls up the sleeves of his shirt and sits down in the chair across from mine.

I wait for him to explain whatever the hell this is, but he just sits back, digs out his phone, and messages someone.

I start to grow restless and annoyed and am about to declare that when a woman enters the building from a side door.

She's wearing a button-down shirt and slacks and looks about ten to fifteen years older than the agent.

"Agent Thomas," she greets the agent as she sits down in a chair beside him.

"Agent Jane," Agent Thomas replies formally without making eye contact.

Tension flows between the two of them, and I wonder why. I also wonder if I can use that to my benefit, maybe play them against each other.

My wheels are turning with ideas when Agent Jane sets a manila folder on the table, along with a flash drive.

My gut tightens at the sight of the flash drive, my mind instantly thinking about what could be on it. The last time someone showed me one of those, it contained a video of me stealing a car. Kyler, Hannah, and Lynn used it to blackmail me into keeping quiet about them taking Isa.

Worry swirls through me.

Is that video on this flash drive? How did these agents get it?

"You look nervous," Agent Jane remarks, observing me. "You don't need to be. Well, as long as you cooperate."

I cross my arms, attempting to appear calmer than I am. "Cooperate about what?"

Agent Jane studies me for a beat then opens the folder and sifts through the papers inside. "You have quite the record for getting in trouble. I see you've been arrested a couple of times, but the charges were always dropped. My bet is your father made that happen." She glances up at me, waiting for an answer, but all I do is shrug. She assesses me for a moment then leans forward, resting her arms on the table and overlapping her hands. "According to Douglas Feriltor, the charges listed in your file are barely anything. That you've committed a lot more crimes than are in your file. Now, usually we don't take the word of a guy who's currently working off a severe list of crimes, but he provided us with some proof that I'm certain will help us start building quite the case against you." She picks up the flash drive.

I resist the urge to swallow hard. "How do I even know what's on it?"

"You don't." She sets the flash drive down. "And that's the appeal of this. It leaves you wondering what evidence we have of the many crimes you've committed."

She's right, and it annoys me. But mostly, I'm annoyed with myself. I wish I could go back in time and not make so many dumbass choices all because I wanted to piss off my dad and Kyler for all the shit they did to me.

"You look worried," Agent Thomas remarks, leaning forward and crossing his arms on the table. "And you should be."

"I'm not," I lie in a lame-ass attempt to get out of this. "I'm just thinking about how lame of a show this is, and I'm wondering what would happen if I just got up and walked out of here, since this isn't an official arrest."

Amusement glints in Agent Jane's eyes as she gestures at the door. "Go ahead and try." She rests back in the chair, looking way too comfortable right after I just threatened to leave.

I'm going to try, though. At least, that's what I tell myself, but then Agent Thomas retrieves a pack of cigarettes from his pocket, and when he opens his jacket, I get a good glimpse of his gun holster and the gun inside it.

The move is completely intentional, and it's enough to keep my ass glued to the chair.

"So, am I going to be arrested?" I ask, confused as to what exactly they want from me.

"We could do that." Agent Jane trades a look with Agent Thomas.

Agent Thomas pops a cigarette into his mouth and lights up, a cloud of smoke circling his face as he exhales. "Or you could help us with a case."

My confusion nearly skyrockets. "Help you how?"

"By working as an informant," Agent Jane replies simply. But what she said is anything but simple.

An informant?

What?

"An informant for what?" I ask, restlessly bouncing my foot up and down. "And don't people who do that usually get ... I don't know, killed?"

Agent Thomas snorts a laugh as he ashes his cigarette. "Just because stuff happens in the movies like that doesn't mean it does in real life."

I lift a brow. "I've read articles about informants getting killed."

He takes another drag off his cigarette. "Even if that's true, for that to happen, the informant probably did something that was off protocol."

I don't believe him. Plus, they haven't even explained what I'd be doing exactly, which makes this whole thing even sketchier.

I'm about to start bombarding them with questions when Agent Jane speaks.

"Until you agree, we can't give you all the details of what case you'll be working," she explains. "However, I will tell you two things. One"—she holds up a finger—"if you don't accept our offer, with the charges we have against, you're looking at five years minimum. And since you're eighteen, you'll serve out that sentence in the state penitentiary."

When I press my lips together, refusing to say anything, she slants forward. "We have records of you hacking into illegal systems. We have video footage of you stealing a car and buying drugs. And we know that your father recently kicked you out of the house, so I highly doubt he'll be there to bail you out this time."

She's right.

I hate that she is.

Honestly, I kind of hate myself at the moment.

"And the second thing I'm going to tell you," she continues, "is that what you'll be doing won't be as risky as what you've seen on TV. You'll simply be working under-cover on the Sunnyvale High School football team."

Okay, that wasn't what I was expecting her to say at all.

"And we've done our research," Agent Thomas adds then takes another drag. "We know that if you wanted to, you could be on the team, that you have in the past, so don't try to use the excuse that you can't get on the team."

"I wasn't going to say that," I lie. I was about to, but I guess I should've known they already knew I used to play football, along with a bunch of other sports, back when I was weak, when I let Kyler torment me, when I lived in his shadow.

I thought I moved past that. And I guess I did, but only to move to this.

Though, I'm still not completely certain what this is.

"What exactly would I be doing?" I ask, fiddling with a leather band on my wrist.

"Like I said, we can't give you all the details until you agree," Agent Jane says.

"But, how can I agree to something when I don't even know what it is?" I point out, frustrated.

"That's the downfall of getting yourself into a position like this." Agent Thomas smirks at me as he puts out his cigarette. "Something you should think about in the future."

"Yeah, but do I even have a future anymore?" I mumble, shaking my head.

"You will as long as you cooperate," Agent Jane insists. "If you do, we'll wipe your record completely clean. And I mean the *entire* thing. Even the charges filed against you two years ago."

I close my eyes as images of two years ago flash through my mind.

I haven't thought about that day in a while, refuse to, but now that she brought it up, it's all I can think about.

"That was an accident," I mutter, opening my eyes.

She shrugs. "Accident or not, a file of it still exists." She holds up the file and the flash drive. "However, if you agree to do this, all of this will be gone."

I grit my teeth until my jaw aches, furious at them, myself, and Big Doug.

Why did he do this to me? Why did he rat me out? The only thing I can think of is that he was trying to buy his own freedom, which just pisses me off more.

But no matter how angry I get, the fact of the matter is that I'm still in this mess. It won't be dissolved by my rage. Rage can't dissolve the past. Nothing can. Even if they get rid of the files on me, what I did and the things done to me will still exist. That doesn't mean I want to go to prison, though. And I could never leave Isa like that. She needs me.

And I need her.

"Fine, I'll do it," I give in. "Now, what exactly do I have to do?"

"Smart answer," Agent Thomas says. "I guess you're not as dumb as your grades make you look."

I don't know about that. Right now, I feel like the dumbest idiot that ever existed.

I had such a good thing going, and I thought it was going to last, that my past wouldn't catch up with me, but I was stupid.

The past always catches up with you.

And the shitty part is that this is just the start of all the things I've been trying to bury.

TEN

ISA

I've been trying to get ahold of Kai for hours, but he won't reply to any of my messages or answer any of my calls. I'm starting to get extremely worried as all sorts of bad scenarios flood my mind. What if T decided to go after him again? What if Lynn and my dad went after him? What if he met up with Big Doug and ...? Well, I don't know how to follow that thought since I'm still not positive what Big Doug does. I believe he is a hacker, but it was never confirmed. That doesn't make him any better.

"I'm worried," I mutter to myself as I pace my bedroom, bursting with restlessness.

Indigo is at work and won't return until tomorrow, and Grandma Stephy has been talking to her boyfriend in the living room for the last two hours, hence the reason I'm in my bedroom.

Sure, Harry is a nice dude and everything, but two of them like to spend a lot of time making out. Usually, they do it in the bedroom, but they decided to hang out in the living room today. I think mainly so she could keep an eye on things.

I sat out there for a while, eating dinner with them and watching the news, but then I saw Harry try to cop a feel of Grandma Stephy when they thought I wasn't looking, so ... yeah, it was definitely time to say *peace out*.

But being by myself has sent me into worry mode.

"I need something sugary," I mumble as I gnaw on my fingernails.

Finally, I decide to woman-up and go to the kitchen to grab a snack.

I leave my bedroom, taking my phone with me, and pad down the hallway. When I reach the doorway to the living room, I clear my throat loudly several times to subtly announce I'm going to enter the room. That way, they'll have time to remove their hands from each other and ... well, do whatever it is they need to do to collect themselves.

"Hey," I say as I enter.

I mentally let out a breath of relief when they smile at me from the sofa with a cushion of space between them and all their clothes on.

"Hey, sweetie," Grandma Stephy replies, looking a bit flushed, something I try to disregard.

Harry gives me a small wave as he pretends to be fixated on the television.

I wave back then hurry into the kitchen and start raiding the cupboards for something to munch on.

"Why are you hiding out in your room?" Grandma Stephy asks as she wanders into the kitchen.

"I'm not," I lie as I open a cupboard. Inside is a box of bran cereal. *Yuck.*

I close the cupboard and move to the next one.

"Don't lie to me, young lady." Grandma Stephy aims for a stern tone but misses the mark. "You're hiding out, and you've been quiet ever since the phone call from your mom." She leans her hip against the counter as she watches me move to the next cupboard. "I think we need to talk about what was said."

"That's not what's bothering me," I insist, which is the partial truth. I'm also worried about Kai. Plus, I can't get that photo out of my mind.

She stares me down with her hawk eyes. "Isabella Anders, don't you dare pull that shit with me. In this house, we tell the truth."

I shut the cupboard and spin around to face her. "Really? Then why don't you tell me what was written on the back of that photo?" When she visibly pales, I feel like a jerk. "I'm sorry." I sigh. "I'm just ... I don't know ..." I let out another sigh then confess, "I saw the photo on your phone."

Her brow curves upward in surprise. "You were snooping?"

"No, I dropped it when I had it earlier and the photo app accidentally opened." I fiddle with the bandage on my wrist. "The girl in it ... she looks so much like me."

Worry flickers in her eyes. "I know, hon."

I smash my lips together and take an inhale then exhale, trying to hold myself together. "Why?"

She shakes her head as she steps toward me. "I'm not sure," she says with remorse. "But the police are doing everything they can to find out."

"Yeah, that's what everyone keeps saying." I give a short pause. "What did the message say?"

She grows even more pale, her lips parting. "It said ..." She trails off as Harry turns up the television volume.

"*Lynn and Henry Anders are considered extremely dangerous,*" the reporter states on the television screen. "*If you have any information about their whereabouts, please call the police department immediately.*" Images of Lynn and my dad appear on the bottom of the screen, along with their descriptions.

Seeing them ...

Hearing this ...

"I need to go to the bathroom," I mutter, hurrying down the hallway.

It's the second time I've used that excuse today. Either I'm starting to look suspicious or everyone probably thinks I have a bladder infection.

"Isa," Grandma Stephy calls after me, but I rush into the bathroom and shut the door.

I stay in there for a while, trying to process what I just saw. But, how do you process seeing your own personal hell splayed across the television for everyone to see?

I wonder how Hannah's handling it. The thought surprises me, but I still wonder. Not that I'm going to call her and ask. Still, I'm betting she's struggling with this, struggling with the fact that everyone in Sunnyvale now knows her life isn't perfect.

As for me? I've dealt with this before. Only, this time I don't have to do it alone. I have my grandma Stephy, Indigo, and Kai.

Speaking of which ...

"Why hasn't he answered any of my messages?" I mutter as I dig out my phone from my pocket.

As if he can somehow hear me, a message from him suddenly pings through.

A ball of pressure leaves my chest as I read it.

Kai: *I'm okay. Some stuff just came up that I didn't*

expect. *I'm heading there now. Everything's okay, though, right?*

Me: *Yeah.* *Well, except for the fact that the news was talking about how Lynn and my dad are wanted fugitives.*

Kai: *I'm so sorry, baby. I'll be there as soon as I can.*

Me: *No, tell Jules to drive the speed limit. I can wait a few extra minutes.*

Kai: *Actually, I'm not with Jules.*

Confusion pulls at my brow.

Me: *Who are you with then?*

Kai: *I can't talk about it via text, but I'll tell you when I get there.*

My confusion morphs into worry.

Me: *You have me a bit worried.*

Kai: *I'm fine.*

Me: *Fine is a placement word.*

About a minute goes by before he replies.

Kai: *I know. I'm just still trying to ... process how I feel about this.*

Me: *About what?*

After a few minutes go by without a response, I exit the bathroom and go back to my room to pace. When another handful of minutes tick by, I decide to raid the candy stash that I keep in my nightstand drawer in an attempt to distract myself. Usually, bingeing on sugar does that for me. Not this time, though.

I'm about one step away from calling Kai when someone knocks on my door.

"Come in," I say as I toss a Snickers wrapper onto my bed.

The door opens and Kai walks in. He looks exhausted and stressed; the dark circles under his eyes have returned, and they also look a bit bloodshot.

The moment I lay eyes on him, I'm overcome with relief.

"I'm so glad you're back," I say as I throw my arms around him.

He slips his arms around my waist and pulls me closer. "Me, too." He nuzzles his face into my hair and breathes in deeply. "God, it's been a shitty day."

His honesty throws me off a bit. Usually, he tries to protect me from having to deal with his issues. What he doesn't realize is it's not something I *have* to do. I *want* to help him.

I pull back and part my lips to ask him what happened, but he talks over me.

"Shhh ... I need something first, and then I'll tell you," he says.

Before I can ask what he needs, he kisses me softly but deeply.

My eyelids lower and, for a brief, wonderful moment, nothing else exists except for him and me and our lips.

Eventually, though, he breaks the kiss and reality returns, pressing down on my shoulders.

He doesn't speak right away, resting his forehead against mine. "I messed up."

I skim my fingers up and down the back of his neck, trying to soothe him. "What happened?"

His breath dusts across my face as he releases a heavy sigh. "All the bad stuff I did in the past, like stealing that car and stuff, finally caught up with me. And now ... well, I have to join the football team and work as an informant to figure out the source of some kind of drug trade going on with the players ... Honestly, there's more to it than that, but I can't really get into the details ... I probably shouldn't even have told you what I just did, but ..." He wraps his hands around my waist and clutches me tightly.

Me? I remain frozen as shock sweeps through me.

"How ...? What ...?" I take a deep breath, trying to collect myself. "How did this happen?"

His grip on my waist tightens. "Big Doug ratted me out. It's why he wanted to meet up with me. There was an agent there and ..." He releases a heavy sigh before pushing me back to look me in the eyes. "I always had this feeling that the shit I did was going to catch up with me. And I know I probably deserve this, but I wish it wasn't happening right now. With everything going on ... you need to be my top priority."

"I'll be fine." Will I, though? Because with that photo and now this ... the walls feel as though they're closing in and I have to remind myself to breathe.

"Hey." Kai cups my cheek as he looks me in the eyes. "You'll be okay. That I can promise you."

"I'm not worried about that right now. I'm worried about you." I loop my arms around the back of his neck, wanting him closer. "This sounds dangerous, and I haven't even heard all of it."

"I'll be fine," he insists.

I shake my head. "Please don't lie to me."

He tucks a strand of hair behind my ear. "I'm not. And honestly, what I have to do, it really shouldn't take that long. I already know a lot of the guys on the team, so all I really need to do is just talk to some people, see who knows what, and then I'll report back to the agents and will be done. Plus, my record will be wiped."

"Really?" I ask, and he nods. Still, worry courses through me. "I'm still worried about you. Drugs? Ratting people out ...? It sounds like some sort of mafia movie."

He cracks a small smile. "I promise you that no one on the football team is in the mafia. It's probably just some player dealing on the side."

"I hope so." I sink into silence as worries for Kai, my life, and that photo overwhelm my mind.

"Where's your head at?" Kai finally asks, searching my eyes.

I lift a shoulder. "I'm still worried about you. And about what's happening with me, too ... I saw the photo Lynn sent. Or, well, allegedly sent."

His eyes widen. "How the hell did you see that?"

I shrug. "It was on my grandma Stephy's phone."

His brow elevates. "Why were you on her phone?"

"Because I was talking to my mom."

Now his brows rise toward his hairline. "Why didn't you say anything?"

"I just did." I let out a sigh. "Plus, I'm still trying to process it ... It was weird ... Talking to her, I mean. And then I saw that photo and I ..." I swallow hard. "Kai, what did the note on the back of it say?"

He shakes his heads. "I don't think—"

"Please, just tell me," I cut him off. "I need to know, or it's all I'm going to think about."

His Adam's apple bobs as he swallows hard. "I don't want to see you hurt ... I mean, I get that not knowing is probably pretty stressful, but I ..." He releases a deafening exhale. "I'll tell you a summarization of what it said, but I refuse to repeat every vile thing that was written on that photo."

I struggle to breathe evenly. "Okay."

He gives a long, hesitant pause. "It basically said that

you'll eventually replace the girl in the photo. That you would hurt like her. That you would suffer for years like her."

My brows pull together. "Suffer for years like her? Why does that sound like that girl has been tied up for years?"

Kai shrugs but tension ripples from him. "I'm not sure, but hopefully, after the police look into it, they'll have some answers." He cups my face with his hands. "But it doesn't even matter, because they'll never get ahold of you. I won't let them. I don't give a shit if I have to be an informant—you'll always come first."

"You always come first with me, too," I say. "But that doesn't mean I want you to constantly worry about me—"

He silences my protest with his lips, kissing me as he backs me up toward the bed.

"Kai," I whisper breathlessly as I work to get out what I need to say.

But he continues to kiss me, refusing to hear it, refusing to let me tell him that I don't want him getting hurt or in trouble for me. That he should put himself first.

We end up kissing until exhaustion overcomes me. I try to keep my eyes open so I can talk to him more, but he smooths his hand over my head and whispers for me to go to sleep.

Eventually, I do.

And for some reason, when I drift into dreamland, I once again end up in that nightmare, in that basement, with that person who is hitting me, which makes me wonder if maybe it's not a nightmare at all, but a memory.

If that's the case, then why am I suddenly remembering?

And why do I get the feeling that, behind the darkness, something horrible is waiting in the corner?

ELEVEN
KAI

I'M NERVOUS ABOUT WHAT I HAVE TO DO, NOT JUST because it's sketchy as hell but because it means I won't be able to keep an eye on Isa all the time. Still, I'll make sure she's safe, no matter what it takes.

That's the promise I'm making to myself as I lie in bed with her, watching her sleep. Her head is resting in the crook of my arm, her lips parted as she softly breathes. I wish I could freeze time and stay right here. Unfortunately, that sort of stuff doesn't exist, something I'm reminded of when my phone vibrates with an incoming message.

I half-expect it to be from the agents, since they told me they'd be in contact with me soon after I left the warehouse and they drove me home.

Jules had texted me at least ten times, wondering

where the hell I went. I had to lie to him, which sucks. But deep down, I know it was only the start of a very long list of lies I'm going to have to tell in the future.

Sighing at that thought, I reach over and pick up my phone. When I see the message is from Kyler, confusion webs through me, but then I read the message and a tiny trace of a smile appears on my lips.

Kyler: *Was it you who planted those drugs in my trunk? I know it was. I can't fucking believe you'd do that to me. You got me kicked off the team, you asshole. I'll never forgive you for this.*

I don't reply, setting the phone down then rolling onto my side and curling into Isa.

At least one good thing happened today. I got revenge for Isa. I just wish I could get revenge for her with Lynn for everything that woman did to her. Maybe one day when she's found, I will. For now, I plan on tormenting Kyler more. And I'm adding someone else to the list.

Hannah Anders, Isa's half-sister. I got big plans for her.

As I close my eyes and start to drift off to sleep with Isa's sugary smell flooding my nostrils, my phone vibrates from the nightstand again. Assuming it's Kyler, bitching me out more, I ignore it. But when it does it again and again, I roll over and pick it up.

Weirdly, it's from Jules.

Jules: *Hey, sorry to message you this late, but I just got some info back on that photo and thought you'd like to know. I ran a facial recognition program on it.*

Jules: *It's actually an illegal program, so you won't be able to report what I'm about to tell you to the police, but I think you need to know.*

Jules: *The program matched the girl's face to Isabella Anders.*

"What the hell?" I mutter, carefully moving my arm out from underneath Isa so I can sit up.

Me: *The program must be shit then, because that's not Isa in that photo.*

Jules: *The program isn't shit. It's actually the best facial recognition program you can get, which is part of the reason why it's illegal, at least to your average citizen. But I understand what you're saying about there being no way Isa could be that girl in the photo. And I knew that when the results came back, so I looked into it and what I found out is that, if the program does match up someone's face to someone else's, ninety-nine percent of the time, it's because they're twins or are related and have very, very similar features.*

I shake my head, completely confused.

Me: *Okay, well, then maybe this is that one percent of the time when the program didn't work correctly.*

Jules: *Maybe. And maybe the police will come up with a better answer. I just thought I'd let you know the results.*

Me: *Thanks. I appreciate you doing this.*

Jules: *Anytime.*

I set the phone down, feeling utterly perplexed over how the program matched Isa's face up wrong.

But the girl in the photo did look so similar that a small part of me wonders if perhaps it could be a relative of Isa's. Maybe that's what it is. Maybe Isa has a cousin who looks almost like her who's helping Lynn out. Then again, Lynn isn't Isa's real mom, so any relatives on her side wouldn't be blood-related to Isa.

Shit, what am I going to do? I can't tell the police about this since Jules will get in trouble, but I feel like they need to know. Maybe I'll get lucky and they'll come up with the same answer.

But luck hasn't been on my side for a while. Well, except for when it comes to Isa being in love with me. That I lucked out on.

And as I lie down in bed beside her, that's what I try to focus on—her.

And for a moment, all my worries go away as I drift off into a peaceful sleep.

I just wish that feeling would last.

ABOUT THE AUTHOR

Jessica Sorensen is a *New York Times* and *USA Today* bestselling author who lives in the snowy mountains of Wyoming. When she's not writing, she spends her time reading and hanging out with her family.

ALSO BY JESSICA SORENSEN

Sunnyvale Series:

The Year I Became Isabella Anders

The Year of Falling in Love

The Year of Second Chances

The Year of Kai and Isa

Untitled (coming soon)

Enchanted Chaos Series:

Enchanted Chaos

Shimmering Chaos

Iridescent Chaos

Untitled (coming soon)

Capturing Magic:

Chasing Wishes

Chasing Magic

Untitled (coming soon)

Chasing the Harlyton Sisters Series:

Chasing Hadley

Falling for Hadley

Holding onto Hadley

Untitled (coming soon)

Cursed Hadley:

Cursed Hadley

Enchanting Hadley (coming soon)

Tangled Realms:

Forever Violet: Everlasting Moonlight

Forever Stardust: Everlasting Stardust

Untitled (coming soon)

Curse of the Vampire Queen:

Tempting Raven

Enchanting Raven

Alluring Raven

Untitled (coming soon)

Unraveling You Series:

Unraveling You

Raveling You

Awakening You

Inspiring You

Fated by Darkness

Untitled (coming soon)

Unexpected Series:

The Unexpected Complications of Revenge

Untitled (coming soon)

Shadow Cove Series:

What Lies in the Darkness

What Lies in the Dark

Untitled (coming soon)

Mystic Willow Bay Series:

The Secret Life of a Witch

Broken Magic

Stolen Kisses

One Wild, Crazy Zombie Night

Magical Whispers & the Undead

Untitled (coming soon)

Standalones:

The Forgotten Girl

Honeyton Annabella:

The Illusion of Annabella

Untitled (coming soon)

Rebels & Misfits:

Confessions of a Kleptomaniac

Rules of a Rebel and a Shy Girl

The Heartbreaker Society:

The Opposite of Ordinary

The Heartbreaker Society Curse

The Heartbreaker Society Secret (coming soon)

Broken City Series:

Nameless

Forsaken

Oblivion

Forbidden (coming soon)

Guardian Academy Series:

Entranced

Entangled

Enchanted

The Forest of Shadow & Bones

Entice

Untitled (coming soon)

The Coincidence Series:

The Coincidence of Callie and Kayden

The Redemption of Callie and Kayden

The Destiny of Violet and Luke

The Probability of Violet and Luke

The Certainty of Violet and Luke

The Resolution of Callie and Kayden

Seth & Greyson

The Evermore of Callie & Kayden

Untitled (coming soon)

The Secret Series:

The Prelude of Ella and Micha

The Secret of Ella and Micha

The Forever of Ella and Micha

The Temptation of Lila and Ethan

The Ever After of Ella and Micha

Lila and Ethan: Forever and Always

Ella and Micha: Infinitely and Always

Untitled (coming soon)

The Shattered Promises Series:

Shattered Promises

Fractured Souls

Unbroken

Broken Visions

Scattered Ashes

Untitled (coming soon)

Breaking Nova Series:

Breaking Nova

Saving Quinton

Delilah: The Making of Red

Nova and Quinton: No Regrets

Tristan: Finding Hope

Wreck Me

Ruin Me

Untitled (coming soon)

The Fallen Star Series:

The Fallen Star

The Underworld

The Vision

The Promise

The Lost Soul

The Evanescence

Untitled (coming soon)

The Darkness Falls Series:

Darkness Falls

Darkness Breaks

Darkness Fades

Untitled (coming soon)

The Death Collectors Series (NA and YA):

Ember X and Ember

Cinder X and Cinder

Spark X and Spark

Untitled (coming soon)

Unbeautiful Series:

Unbeautiful

Untamed

Untitled (coming soon)

27753567R00080

Printed in Great Britain
by Amazon